# ❧❧ The GHASTLING ❧❧

GHASTLING
Nº 08

At the Witching
Hour of
Midnight

The

Ghastling

Nº 08

HALLOWEEN

# The *Ghastling*
## BOOK Nº VIII

Book Number Eight, Cardiff, Wales, 2018

# GHASTLING EDITORIAL STAFF

EDITOR
Rebecca Parfitt

ASSISTANT EDITOR
Rhys Owain Williams

ART DIRECTOR
Nathaniel Winter-Hébert

ADVISER
Maria J. Pérez Cuervo

SPECIAL THANKS TO
Leona Preston, M.S. Corley, J&C Parfitt

DESIGN
Winter-Hébert

CONTACT
editor@theghastling.com
theghastling.com
facebook.com/theghastling

GRATITUDE TO PATRONS
Chip Limeburner & Trevor Murray
(If you would like to become a patron too please visit:
*patreon.com/TheGhastling*)

ISBN NO  978-0-9934991-5-9
ISSN  2514-815X

*The Ghastling gratefully acknowledges
the financial support of the* WELSH BOOKS COUNCIL.

# EDITORIAL *by* Rhys Owain Williams

IT MAY NOT come as much of a surprise, but autumn is our favourite season. With all of the possibilities of summer gone, and the chill of winter on the horizon, autumn is a time for celebrating the dark: observing the traditions of All Hallows' Eve and the ancient festival of Samhain.

Though similar festivals are held at this time of the year across other Celtic lands, the Gaelic festival of Samhain is perhaps the most well known. For the Celts, Samhain was the equivalent of New Year's Eve, marking the end of one year and the beginning of the next. The Celtic calendar saw new days begin at sunset, rather than midnight, and so a new year began as soon as darkness hit. This was a liminal time, when the boundary between this world and the otherworld was at its thinnest, and could more easily be crossed.

We wanted the stories we chose for this issue of *The Ghastling* to reflect the traditions of this season, both ancient and modern. The festival of Samhain begins on the Gregorian date of October 31st, a date that now conjures up thoughts of ghost stories, costume parties and trick-or-treating. The celebration of Halloween is several centuries old itself, but it's widely believed that many of its traditions originated from the much older Samhain.

Among these peculiar traditions is the carving of vegetable lanterns with grotesque faces. In Damien B Raphael's story THE SCULPTURE, an artisan suggests that the flesh of a pumpkin is far more forgiving for this type of work than the more traditional turnip – but what exactly has he been commissioned to carve in his dimly-lit studio?

Grinning, hand-carved faces light the town in Catrin Kean's FOGTIME, as children in bedsheets run from door to door swinging rattling buckets. Dressing up as someone else – or some*thing* else – and demanding treats is another odd custom that we've grown to accept as part of the season. This too is traced to the Celts, who were said to leave offerings of food and drink to placate the fairies, witches, demons and unfortunate souls who wandered between this world and the next on Samhain. Perhaps it isn't just the young trick-or-treaters, then, that make Mammy lock the doors and pull the curtains.

In Alys Hobbs' IN WE COME, it's adults who roam the streets disguised – a troupe of actors, to be exact, searching for an audience for their folk play. "Make room, for in we come! We've come a-mumming, three-two-one!" However, this troupe's antics seem to go beyond mere performance, and it may not just be money or

food that they're looking for in exchange.

The Celts believed that the sun began to grow weak during Samhain, and so bonfires were lit not just in honour of the dead, but also to guide them on their journey – and keep them away from the living. So when Jenny watches a constellation of flickering lights appear on Kristy Kerruish's THE HILL, she should probably keep a safe distance – but Trevor has been gone for a while, and it's all mumbo-jumbo anyway... isn't it? Mr Fanner certainly hopes not, as he walks AMONG OCTOBER'S FIELDS with the derelict Riverbrook Home for Boys in his sights. Callum McKelvie's story begins with whispers: the tragic fire, all the children gone and mysterious sounds across the fields at night. Mr Fanner is searching for inspiration for his next ghost story, but he may wish that he had looked elsewhere.

Leaving the restless bonfires of Samhain behind, let's instead turn to the quietness of the fireside, where storytelling has long been the preferred form of entertainment. At Halloween, the attention of the fireside storyteller unsurprisingly turns to ghosts and the macabre, and so we felt it was important to include a selection of tales that, if not specifically Halloween-themed, were befitting of this seasonal tradition. So read aloud if you dare the DIARY OF A DEADMAN by N. A. Wilson, follow Mark Sadler into the sweltering woods in THE POACHER'S BALL and enter Florence Vincent's THE TEMPLE to experience foreboding in a foreign land. Then, we suggest you gather friends around the campfire to share HOW SHADOWS FALL, C. L. Hanlon's fresh take on the legend of the vanishing hitchhiker.

Samhain marks the beginning of the darker half of the year, and there is darkness in the pages that follow. So lock the door, draw the curtains and light that jack-o'-lantern. We'll see you on the other side...

# The POACHER'S BALL

## by Mark Sadler

WE HAD rambled for almost three hours into fading winter light, across a rustic landscape of small woods and pasture that was lapsing to wilderness. The buckled contour lines of old tillings, now overrun with scrub, hinted at long abandoned attempts at raising crops. I began to feel, in the pit of my belly, the gnawing panic of a man who knows himself to be lost and at the mercy of a stranger.

In single file we entered one of the wooded areas. I had seen it from the snarled summit of an earthen ridge we had occupied only a few minutes before. We had paused there momentarily, gazing downhill across a sunken carpet of wild brush that clung to the jumbled topography of an old landslip. A dry fog, reminiscent of the dispersing smoke of a recent fire, appeared to linger along the fringes of the thicket and in the air above the still heads of the trees.

The encroaching dusk had already colonised the dark spaces underneath the pale boughs. Abbott – who was the master of this interminable estate – had paused ahead of me at a junction between the ghostly, upright-slanting columns of the blanched trunks, where two meandering trails of dead leaves crossed over. Handicapped by my long-absent lung, I laboured to draw level with him.

"This wood has a natural direction," he announced from the gloom. "It wants to advance to the east; to return perhaps to its point of origin, however circumstances prevent it from doing so. We are walking towards the west and against the prevailing grain of the landscape."

The crooked pathway was crowded on either side by wild, un-pruned trees, each one a copse of its own making, issuing from the ground as an untidy spray of thick branches that fanned almost straight upwards. Through the spindly winter thatch overhead, static, leaden clouds smouldered with the orange-red glow of a hidden sunset. As I, at last, caught up with my guide, the tinted light conspired to fall upon him in such a manner that the most malevolent aspects of his features were thrown into stark relief, and he assumed an almost demonic air.

Since we had entered the woodland, the

temperature had been rising steadily and now approximated an unseasonal mid-summer swelter. While Abbott appeared unaffected by it, I was flushed and sweating underneath the layers of heavy clothing that I had donned in anticipation of the evening chill.

"This heat; it feels like it comes from all around us," I panted.

Abbott observed my exertions with an expression of blank disinterest that was entirely void of empathy.

"The cause is no great mystery, Mr Heald. As we stand here and take our rest, the forest is burning down around us. Kindly indulge me by touching one of the trunks."

I placed the flat of my hand against an expanse of rough white bark. A living warmth seemed to circulate beneath the surface. Flickering pinpricks of concentrated heat danced across my palm as if the points of small flames were lapping at my skin. Hastily I withdrew and inspected myself for signs of burns. There were none.

"I say. It's rather hot."

"I have brought you to the earliest part of the grounds, to a grove of half-tone ash that is many thousands of years old. Where the sunlight penetrates through fault-lines in the bark, it kindles the sap. The inferno that rages inside these trees has burned since long before you were born. It once kept rising waters at bay when all around here was flooded."

I scoffed at him: "Well, I don't see how that can be possible."

"The fire was set deliberately by my father. It was one of a great many conditions that he levied against me, prior to passing on ownership of the estate. In truth it was of no more use to him. He had long ago taken his leave of the place. Through his absence and neglect it had fallen to the state that you see now. Before this was unkempt woodland it used to be an orchard garden with a roaming menagerie of animals and a great tree that stood at the centre. In another age it will be a mountain of ash."

"Better to chop it all down then, what?" I remarked jovially. "Sell the timber."

A stiff tremor passed between the dry, quivering branches of the slow-kindling trees, as if they were collectively shuddering in anticipation of the bite of the woodsman's axe.

"When these trees are gone, Mr Heald, their ashes will be worth more than all of the gold in all of the world's vaults. They are the fundamental materials of creation, from which all things have, and will be, made. A thimblefull could restore the most barren and forsaken desert to a paradise. A time will come when men will crawl upon their bellies and debase their divine nature in exchange for the barest pinch."

"Well, they haven't done much for this old place so far," I muttered.

Beneath his moustache, Abbott's lips tightened. A flicker of anger came and went behind his eyes. It was the first time that I had witnessed in him any semblance of emotion. I attempted a conciliatory gesture that emerged as an exasperated flaring of my hands.

"I am terribly sorry, Mr Abbott. I am your guest and I forget myself. Please do not mistake my extreme tiredness for an absence of decorum, but..."

At this point my breath became suddenly short, as it often does since my illness.

"...But I have travelled a great distance... and we have been walking for what seems like an eternity... And I fail to see what any of this has to do with the purpose of my visit... If you please, I should rather like to return to the house... via the shortest possible route... and

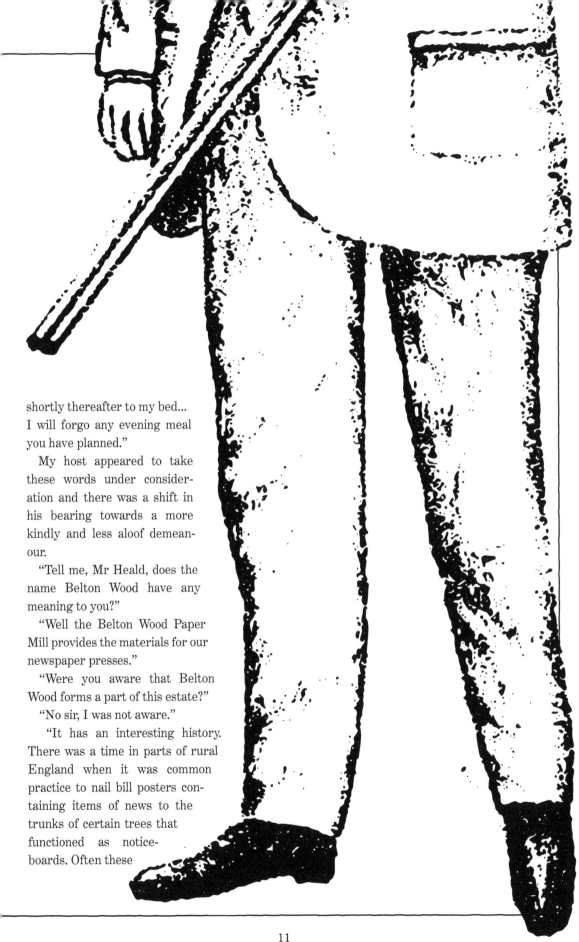

shortly thereafter to my bed...
I will forgo any evening meal
you have planned."

My host appeared to take
these words under consider-
ation and there was a shift in
his bearing towards a more
kindly and less aloof demean-
our.

"Tell me, Mr Heald, does the
name Belton Wood have any
meaning to you?"

"Well the Belton Wood Paper
Mill provides the materials for our
newspaper presses."

"Were you aware that Belton
Wood forms a part of this estate?"

"No sir, I was not aware."

"It has an interesting history.
There was a time in parts of rural
England when it was common
practice to nail bill posters containing items of news to the
trunks of certain trees that
functioned as notice-
boards. Often these

were venerable oaks that stood close to a blacksmiths where the hammers and nails necessary for the task could be procured. Belton Wood in Essex was once home to over thirty such trees. Over time an informal stewardship of the area saw different trees devoted to different types of news – weddings, obituaries, news from beyond the outlying villages and so forth. This repository of information eventually coalesced into The Belton Herald – one of the country's earliest newspapers. I believe it was acquired by your paper a decade ago and closed down a year after."

"Yes, yes I recall... The editor at the time was my predecessor, Monty Gaudan."

"It appears to be something of a surprise to you that I supply the raw materials for your printing presses, as I do for many of the newspapers in England. I do hope that it will not be regarded as a conflict of interest."

"Let me assure you sir, your provision of blank paper will never be allowed to exert any influence upon the words that we elect to print upon it."

My rebuttal appeared to invoke some private amusement in Abbott, sufficient enough to spur him to address the purpose of my visit.

"You first wrote to me in December of last year enquiring after the late sportsman, Sir Robin Gager. The spot where we presently stand is where he began his career. The date of our meeting corresponds to the date when he and I first made an acquaintance, though I knew something of him before that time.

"Before Gager was a cricketer, he was poacher. This place was a faerie wood then. He crept over my fences at night to pilfer will-o'-wisps from my land. These recidivist acts of petty theft brought him neither happiness, nor any great wealth. He sold his ill-gotten gains for a pittance to wreckers on the Cornish coast. I understand, in that part of the country, they train faerie lights to lure passing ships onto rocks.

"It is a long time since I have seen any wisps in the woods. I recall them being hard to catch. Their only natural predators were the goshawks. A man would close his hand around one, only to find that it had slipped past his fingers in the last moment. Gager used to knock them out of the air with a cricket ball. As I have said, it was a meagre living and he harboured secret ambitions elsewhere.

"He came out here one night, with his ball and his sack. I was waiting for him alone, as I stand before you now. After he had been convinced that I bore him no ill will, and we had come to an understanding in regard to the true purpose of our meeting, I asked of him what he wanted most in life. A year and a day after our meeting he was inducted into the English cricket team."

"And you claim that you were his sponsor? Or the man who perhaps, through his influence, cleared the path for his ascent?"

"In a manner of speaking. Gager was no gentleman and had no footing in polite society prior to my involvement. Under my patronage and tutelage, he developed an underhand style of bowling that proved effective in stealing wickets. He was despised by many in the establishment for it. They claimed that he had brought something disreputable from his old profession into the game; a stain on the reputation of the sport that could never be fully expurgated.

"His personal success was marred by a string of memorable failures. He stood briefly, bat in hand, before the pale wicket at the Oval in 1882, where England were bested by Australia. After the match, I sent him an urn containing some of the ashes from this wood, as a reminder of our agreement. He had it inscribed and turned into a trophy that has been passed back and forth between the two rival nations ever since, though that was not the true purpose of my gift: Men who have risen quickly, and in such a manner that defies explanation, must occasionally be reminded that their ascent did not occur unaided, and

that what has been given can as easily be taken away."

Abbott removed a spherical bulge from the side pocket of his jacket. Drawing back his left arm, he hurled it with great force at one of the trees. They was a sharp crack, followed by a dazzling eruption of white flame that died in an instant to a fierce crackle, lingering on the air like the sound of a fire spitting fat. The smouldering husk of a ruptured cricket ball wobbled to a full-stop on the gloomy mosaic of fallen leaves, halting a few inches short of Abbott's immaculately polished shoes.

"Historically this is a place where men come to yield to their temptations and give form to their desires. I must respectfully ask you, Mr Heald, what is it that you want, beyond your eagerness to learn more of Mr Gager for your newspaper article, of course?"

He regarded me with hard searching eyes that seemed to breach my innermost defences and bore down into the very core of my essence.

"If that question perturbs you, then ask of yourself: What is the one thing I lack and that I wish to define me?"

I felt a surge of desire welling in my chest, as if the answer was being drawn out of me by some natural action of the body; my tongue moving to form the shape of words, and my lips moving in partnership to give them voice.

A sudden patter of heavy rain stampeded overhead. The steaming woodland hissed at the darkening skies like a coiled snake holding an interloper at bay.

# THE SCULPTURE
## *by* Damien B. Raphael

**M**RS HALL stood shivering in a paved, narrow garden of an unkempt lodging house, inspecting her employee's work. She watched with twitchy eyes, underneath the brim of her umbrella, as he knelt by a virgin patch of chestnut coloured earth, raking his hands across the dirt.

"This is hardly the garden I pictured," said Mrs Hall, "hardly the neighbourhood at all, for such things."

Her artisan, Mr Foley, stood up and stretched his broad frame, rain trickling off his spattered frock coat. "'Tis not the earth that makes it, ma'am," he said, flashing her a grin, more gums than teeth. He adjusted his kerchief. Mrs Hall smiled back, pretending not to taste the tang of his stench, but her eyelid betrayed her and fluttered.

"I suppose you shall be needing these?" Mrs Hall dipped into her chatelaine bag and pulled out a small drawstring bundle, shaking it in Foley's direction. "Sailed across the Atlantic, and delivered this morning. Hopefully, the effort won't be in vain." Silently, Foley took it from her, untied it, and fished out a dusty pellet, a seed no bigger than a tooth.

"It won't," he said. "Nothing I've carved can compare. Not for faces, anyway."

Mrs Hall nodded. "Will you be needing new tools? I'll gladly purchase them from a shop in town."

"No. For this, I'll use what's available. Sticks, pocketknives, pins, doesn't matter. The skill isn't in them, it's in these." He clenched his hands into fists, all but squishing what was in his palm, and brandished the two hunks of meat like a pugilist. Mrs Hall tilted her face upwards, her spine as straight as a billiard cue. The intimidation was not to be intimated.

Mr Foley got to work. Pressing a fat thumb into the middle of the patch of earth, he dropped the seed into the little hole of his making. And conjuring a needle that had been fastened to an inner lapel, he began to speak quickly and quietly, rushed incantations of dark peculiarities, as he inserted the needle into his dirty finger, the blood weeping out and into the ground, soaking against the husk.

Mrs Hall looked away, such heathen mischief too much altogether, and studied Mr Foley's lodging house. It had grown grimmer in the short time of her visit, darker against the cast-iron grey clouds that had amassed over London. And but for a candle in the window of Mr Foley's room, which doubled as his studio, it would have appeared uninhabited altogether. Strange for such a house, really, as either side of it were similar brick-built hovels – yet crammed with paupers who had barely enough room to sneeze. It was as if Mr Foley's house had been damned, a place where few dared to tread. For Mrs Hall, though, it was a must, considering her circumstances. That cold spring morn was the first time she'd visited his lodg-

ings, the first time she'd witnessed what those hands could truly muster. She had stepped into his dimly lit studio tentatively, only to knock over something. Cursing, Mr Foley had lit a tallow candle, then scanned the flame across each and every sculpture, shadows skittering off noses, chins and ears, the likenesses of which had caused Mrs Hall to draw breath, so certain was she they were actual people pretending to be dead. The very nature of the wood, the grain, the hardness, had seemingly melted into skin and wrinkles and warts, faces anchored in agonies and lamentations, rendered with such divine skill, they would have been equal to any marble in Rome, but for their poses. She had asked where he had trained. He'd shaken his head. She had asked of any exhibitions. He'd merely laughed. Uneasily, she'd looked around the room once more, and after gulping, dry-mouthed, inquired about her own commission. Such work, he'd told her, could only be made from something edible. He had had success with the humble turnip in the past, even swedes and carrots, but found the carving of them difficult and not to his liking. The flesh of a pumpkin was far more forgiving.

After Mr Foley had finished in the garden, he chaperoned Mrs Hall through the hostile streets of his neighbourhood, past the glare and altercations outside gin palaces, and back into the gaslit safety of the main thoroughfare of Cornhill. Before descending into Bank station, formerly the crypt of St Mary Woolnoth, she turned quickly and offered Mr Foley a folded clipping of newsprint.

Mr Foley peeled it open. It was a review from a theatrical magazine, alongside a picture of an actress dressed in costume; her velvet hat laden with uncurled ostrich feathers.

"Her sister lives a stone's throw from Westminster, her address is—"

"When Samhain fast approaches, delivery will be assured." Foley carefully folded the paper again. "And if it satisfies you – to inspect how I'll be getting along – you'll always be welcome at my door. Just knock."

"Well…" Mrs Hall feigned a smile, words failing her. Nothing could be worse than visiting that den of simulation again. She tipped her head, disappearing into the station. Mr Foley waited until she was out of sight and, placing the newsprint on his tongue like holy communion, gulped it down.

The underground train swept Mrs Hall across London, away from the dreariness of the east, and the figures standing in that backroom, back to her flat on Upper Cheyne Row.

Mrs Hall ascended the stairwell leading up to her dwellings slowly, the night air affecting her knees. And when at last she bolted and locked the front door, lighting gaslamps to banish any inch of darkness, she began to shiver but not from the cold, rather from the fact she'd actually gone through with meeting Mr Foley. Without supper, she retired to her bedroom, and laid down on her bed and closed her eyes, only to fidget and worry well into the wee hours. When sleep did eventually arrive, Mrs

Hall dreamt of something awful, a sluggish wound growing on her arm, her body frozen to the mattress.

Next morning Mrs Hall had a visitor. As she was getting dressed the doorbell rang making her start and, sleepily, hobble to the front door and open it for her guest, Pip Whitaker – the very reason for her visit to Mr Foley. Miss Whitaker brushed past her, bounding inside and glanced around the flat. "You look dreadful, Mrs Hall. Whatever have you been up to?"

"Welcome, Pip. I'll put the kettle on, do make yourself at home."

It had been a year since their acquaintanceship had soured, a rapport that had started off amicably enough. Pip had sought out Mrs Hall's help from an advert in a local newspaper. And, at first, she was taken in with Mrs Hall's gift, what with so many correct guesses – closer to the truth than any other medium she'd visited. But as her newfound seeress began to charge ever more increasing sums to contact her former twin, Lucy, Pip had grown suspicious. So much so, in fact, that Pip had decided to follow her on occasion, curious to see where all the money was being spent. Mrs Hall's routine had been rather prosaic, apart

CLAIRVOYANTS.

# EVA FAY
## WOMAN
## OF MYSTERY
## 3501 Olive St.

# CLAIRVOYANCY
### AND CONSULT THE GREAT

from certain days, when she'd spend her time in the reading room of the British Museum, or in the British Library, the latter having the most complete archive of newspapers in the country. And, on one rainy afternoon, after keeping close tabs on her, Pip had requested the library clerk to fetch the newspapers Mrs Hall had been perusing in particular. It was no shock as to which. For Pip's sister had lived her life on the stage, treading the boards at the Lyceum Theatre until her untimely death, and the so-called medium had simply been poring over interviews and gossip concerning Pip's dearly departed. Mrs Hall was nothing more than a charlatan, a careless one at that, spoon feeding a jumble of facts to her sitter, as if they'd been plucked from the very ether itself. After the revelation, Pip had played along for a while, gleeful in Mrs Hall's unwitting deceit, which culminated in a séance held at Pip's house in Pimlico. Halfway through the performance, Pip had let go of the dummy's hand – the prosthetic hand masquerading as Mrs Hall's own – and switched on a battery-operated torch, light spewing out of its

bulls-eye glass lens. Mrs Hall had cried out in alarm, one for having never seen such a device, and two for being found out, but by then it was already too late. She'd been caught red-handed holding a tambourine, mid tap – a spirit message of mundane origin.

Afterwards, in the weeks that had followed, Pip had designed ways of exacting revenge, though what exactly that should entail, she could never really decide. Undeterred in her lack of planning, Pip would appear out of the blue at Mrs Hall's home, sometimes for lunch, sometimes for dinner, making only idle chit-chat. Mrs Hall would always respond, guardedly. Respectfully. Knowing no other means to support herself, the vague threat of Pip's presence, and the knowledge she possessed, became a hacksaw against Mrs Hall's nerves. And when Pip had begun to ask to borrow money, in ever increasing amounts, the tables had truly turned. Within half a year, Mrs Hall had estimated, she would be forced out of her flat. Perhaps even into a lodging house.

Listening to Pip ramble on in the parlour, Mrs Hall stirred the tea, adding a splash of milk. *And perhaps*, Mrs Hall thought, *a dash of rat poison, too? Or even a few drops of laudanum to dull her senses, and a glass paperweight to the head?* But then there was the body to consider. Pip wasn't large, yet she possessed a strong physique, weighing ten stones at least. Mrs Hall could barely manage hefting her groceries up the several flights of stairs, let alone a full-grown adult. No, it would be too difficult that way.

Mrs Hall set the tea on a table beside Pip, and took up a seat herself, close to the fireplace.

"Terrible weather, isn't it?" said Pip.

"Unseasonably cold," replied Mrs Hall.

"And how's the business? Don't suppose the weather affects it much, being indoors and all that."

Mrs Hall set down her teacup and took in a deep breath. "I want to talk to you, about a serious matter."

Pip watched on with a glint in her eye.

"Business is terrible," said Mrs Hall. "My regulars have all but abandoned me. Word of mouth will tend to do that, I suppose."

Pip shrugged. "No smoke without fire."

"I am truly sorry," said Mrs Hall much too quickly. "Truly I am. For taking advantage. And, I… believe I've found a way to make it up to you." Pip's eyes never left Mrs Hall, her jaw imperceptibly clenching. "I've been in contact with someone," continued Mrs Hall. "He isn't a medium, or a psychic per se. In truth, I don't know what he is. Only that he is very skilled, and his work is legitimate. And very expensive. And if you wish to connect with your sister—"

"You have insulted my sister's memory, and you think insulting it again would appease me?"

"His work is genuine."

"Work? What type of work?"

"Invocation," said Mrs Hall. "I've wagered half of my savings that he can help you, say goodbye."

Pip's loathing towards Mrs Hall had calcified long ago, but in that moment something inside her had loosened, a thread of hope unravelling her stubbornness. "If it's more seances and table tipping, then it shan't be of interest."

"No," said Mrs Hall. "Nothing of the sort. But he can help. I've seen it, first hand. And oddly enough, I do believe him."

Pip scoffed. She picked up her gloves, fussing over them, and with a look of contempt, left Mrs Hall sitting alone in the drawing room, as a long case clock chimed quarter past.

Mrs Hall never spoke to Pip about the matter again, not once in all her sporadic visits over the following months. But she knew that it was too late to go back on her word with Mr Foley, and she could only wait the summer out.

And it was a cold, bleak summer, even for England. It was as if the weather had conspired to stunt all things that grew, as if the clime itself knew something was gestating which had no right to.

Mr Foley inspected the garden every day, tending to the patch as if it were sacred. He weeded it once in the morning, once in the evening, and watered it constantly with a collection of tin cans he used to collect up rainwater, though the earth never seemed to be sated.

The pumpkin grew to an incredible size, just inches shy of Mr Foley's hip, its skin as orange as marmalade. On the first of October, Mr Foley deemed it ready to begin his work. He sliced the flesh into pieces easier to manoeuvre and lugged them up to his studio, one by one, one blustery night. And, in the reddish light of a grease lamp, he got to work, a profuse sweat

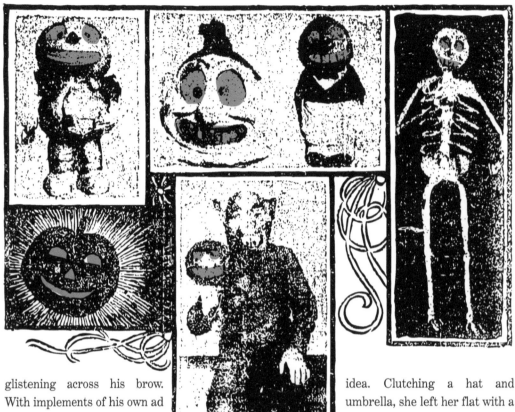

glistening across his brow. With implements of his own ad hoc creation, needles bound against blunt pencils with string, he began to carve quickly and methodically, barely looking at the sculpture itself, his salmon-pink, bloated eyes fixed in distant reverie.

By the middle of October, Miss Whitaker's visits to Chelsea had all but stopped.

At this, Mrs Hall grew ever more pensive, left alone in her flat to stew in worry and the ever-encroaching dark of autumnal evenings. She had thought of visiting Mr Foley, but every time she had gotten ready, she couldn't quite manage to unlock the door, deciding instead on writing a letter she'd put off penning, or making a tea, to warm her for the journey, a journey that would never come. It continued like this for days, always pretending that the next effort to visit Spitalfields really would be the decisive one, when Mrs Hall had had an idea. Clutching a hat and umbrella, she left her flat with a purposeful stride and boarded an omnibus to London Victoria, and once there, walked the rest of the short distance to Pimlico.

Pip's street was a shabby one, lined with terraces blasted by the soot and dust of the burgeoning metropolis. Yet Pip's home, however, was well maintained, perhaps the best-presented house on the street, its front door gleaming with a fresh coat of cyan paint. Mrs Hall stood outside, holding on to the iron grating. There was candlelight in one of the uppermost windows, dyed wine red by strips of stained glass, drops of rain splatting against its mottled surface. She approached the front door, tapped the doorknocker, and pressed the brass medallion bell push for good measure too. No sound stirred from within. Undaunted, Mrs Hall peeked through the letterbox. The hallway was a murky, shadowy grey. She stepped back, looking up to the window with the light, only to hear the front door unlock and, looking down, caught the sallow face of Miss Whitaker receding into the gloom, wordlessly. Mrs Hall licked her dried lips, folded her umbrella and shook off the rain, stepping inside. Pip was nowhere to be seen.

"Miss Whitaker?" she said, closing the door.

Her voice was greeted with silence. Placing her umbrella in a stand, she inched forwards. In the dimness, she could just perceive the hallway was very sparse, the walls bare and empty. There was a sound in the parlour, the breaking of glass. Mrs Hall went to the parlour door, pushing it open.

It was as dark as the hallway, but for a roaring fire. Miss Whitaker sat beside it, her face pale and clammy. Littered around her were piles of photograph albums, photograph frames, each one emptied of their sentimental treasure.

Silently, Mrs Hall watched Pip tear a photograph from the album in her lap, and drop it into the fire, the paper bubbling into flames. Mrs Hall stepped closer. Some of the remnants of the photographs that Miss Whitaker had burnt had fallen out, onto the tiled fireplace. In one charred picture, the face of her twin could be seen, half melted.

"Pip?" said Mrs Hall. But without answering, Miss Whitaker simply discarded another photograph into the fire. Mrs Hall reached over and placed her hand on Pip's shoulder. She shivered, looking up at her visitor.

"The bedroom," said Pip, with a quizzical look.

Mrs Hall left her to her work and ascended the stairwell.

It was at the first door she happened upon what Pip had alluded to.

The bedchamber was small, and well-lit with many candles. The four-poster bed that hogged most of the space was far too big for the room and certainly far too big for the house. Curtains were drawn around it, veiling whoever lay within.

Something whispered behind them.

Mrs Hall, trying to bluster her way through a quickening heartbeat, demanded whoever it was to speak. But the air remained answerless. And on a sudden reflex of courage, she tore the curtain aside, revealing who the sleeper was.

Mr Foley's sculpture was realistic even by his standards.

Pip's twin had been remade, fully formed, arms and limbs, ears and teeth, her body clothed in a nightgown – possibly her own. Mrs Hall trembled, clutching her hands across her belly and silently bore witness to the diabolism, finding it impossible to unglue her eyes from the grotesquery. Every possible aspect of Lucy's form was handled with astonishing detail. The wrinkles on the soles of her feet. The veins in her hands, hands that were twisted together, as if in prayer to the devil himself. And her expression. It was tortured. Defiled. Unholy. Lucy's eyes had been hollowed out, and in the cavities behind them flickered the light of more candles, their glow compounded by the orangeness of the pumpkin's innards. Spindles of wax leaked down her face in a mockery of tears.

"He said never to let them go out." Mrs Hall jumped at Pip's remark, unaware she'd been standing beside her. "He said, most don't like coming back, that it causes them pain. But isn't our pain, the pain of the living, more real?"

Pip moved into the room, sat down on the creaking bed, and snuggled up to Lucy, caressing her sister's carven hands. The flesh of the pumpkin sweated, squidging at her touch. The very first inklings of rot.

Mrs Hall fled the bedchamber.

Down the stairs, into the street.

And hurried back home.

# DIARY
# OF A DEAD MAN

## *by* N.A. Wilson

THE ACCOUNT OF WHICH I am about to tell you has only recently come to light here in the library of good friends of my family; being somewhat of an historian they thought that several items would be of interest to me. So here I sit late into the night, fascinated by a pair of assegai spears adorning the wall and the tale of an ancestor who died some thirty-four years ago in this very house. His name was Charles Baxter, the year of his death being 1903.

I presume you have all heard of Doctor Livingstone and his famous exploits in Africa. But few, I deem, would be aware of the existence of a diary he kept that spanned the six-month period prior to his death. The hunt for this diary has become a passion of mine; an item that academia should have rejoiced in, and yet within days of its discovery, it dwindled from the minds of all those who knew of its existence. A veil of utter secrecy descended as swiftly as a snuffed-out candle.

**I HAVE HUNTED** out the man servant and his good lady wife who nursed Livingstone through the last years of his life. My cover is to pose as an antiquarian, primarily looking for African artefacts, having read every book on the subject with a passion.

From what I have been able to ascertain about James MacCready, he is a pleasant and most likeable fellow. His wife, Emily, is no beauty, having not the delicate features of a lady, but one who has had to work hard over many years. Her kindness to strangers is surpassed only by her devotions to God and her husband in that order.

To this end I have brought my Bible with me and a pair of shoes made by MacCready's father in the hopes that they might ease my acquaintance. I have also taken a room at the King James of Scotland Inn; James MacCready sometimes visits this establishment, usually when his wife is entertaining her sister who comes to stay regularly on her way down to Edinburgh.

## KING JAMES OF SCOTLAND INN:
### late October
A man approached me dressed in a well-tailored tweed suit. "James Mac-Cready," he said, as we shook hands. "Charles Baxter," I returned, gesturing for him to sit in the high-backed chair opposite.

"I understand, sir, that you are interested in African history?"

"I am, sir." I casually tapped out my pipe on the heel of my shoe to draw attention to it.

"They were made by my father – there's his maker's mark," he pointed to where the sole met the heel.

As we drank, we talked. I think that he found in me someone who he could confide in – the intimacy of strangers, I believe it is called. As he was getting up to leave he invited me to dinner the following evening at seven. I gratefully accepted.

**THE MUTTON WE** ate was tasty and went down well with the roast potatoes for which I am a glutton. I brought the topic of conversation towards Livingstone and they were quite happy to inform me of their previous employer and his exploits.

"I had to sort out Livingstone's effects. Most of the items were sent to various universities and museums, but there was one trunk – made you feel uneasy, like you were trespassing on someone's memories. It held only a few clothes and some scorched diary pages."

"And what happened to those?" I asked, the words tumbling out.

"The trunk and two assegai spears went to Professor Patterson at Edinburgh University, the diary pages went on display there, but I believe they disappeared. It caused quite a fuss at the time."

I became aware that Emily was repeating herself. "As I was trying to tell you, Mr Baxter, there are other pages."

"Please forgive me, my mind was gathering wool. Am I right in assuming you have these in your possession?"

"Why yes. My sister has been collecting the other items back together for Professor Patterson. She will take the pages there tomorrow."

The large brown envelope contained only six charred pages, ineptly torn from a diary. I placed them out upon the bed as I sat beside them, the tops burnt away leaving no date or any reference that I could make out. The writing became less sure of its conviction as the entries continued, often indecipherable through fading and foxing of the paper:

'– a gift of such generosity could not go unanswered – tribal chieftain happy to see me – I cannot for the life of me work out what this thing is, I accepted it in all good faith but I wonder what this – I visited the village again today – the witch doctor smiled, perhaps the animosity between us is gone – a black shadow and a feeling of unease – I am feeling unwell again – The gift that they gave me is no gift – The chieftain will not take back the – My man servant has left me, he will not enter the tent with the thing –

I buried it tonight by the light of the moon, the stench is getting worse – ill again, I am keeping little down – I saw it again last night, on the morrow I will – Someone must have dug it up! – I am cursed by it, never free of it – claws at my leg, I am going mad – crawls along the floor — I have packed everything in my chest, I leave with my guide on the morrow – I have left instructions as to where to send –'

I read the entries again, trying to fill in the gaps. If anything, these few half-sentences only intrigued me more. I resolved to determine how many other diary pages had been donated to the university and made a copy of the entries for my own notes. I was meticulous in my detail, filling in single letters where possible.

**ARRIVING AT THE** MacCreadys' home, I met Millicent Grey, Emily's sister, staying here on her way down to Edinburgh. Millicent had been a librarian at Inverness University where she had made the acquaintance of Stephen Patterson, Professor of African Studies at Edinburgh University. She was now helping him compile a comprehensive catalogue of all things African. I asked if I could accompany her to Edinburgh, finding that Miss Grey was delighted to have a travelling companion.

## A Splendid Trophy

**ON ALL HALLOWS' EVE**, I escorted Millicent along labyrinthine corridors at the university. Finally, we came to a large door bearing the words in gold letters, 'Professor Stephen Patterson, Chair of African Studies'. Millicent knocked before a voice said "Come."

"Millicent, my dear . . . I was not expecting you until tomorrow."

"This is Mr Baxter."

Noticing me for the first time, the Professor shot me a steely glance.

"Professor Patterson, how do you do?" I shook his hand warmly. "Charles Baxter, what a wonderful collection you have here."

"Oh, do you think so? This is only a small part of it. Are you interested in Africa at all?"

I talked at length, in fact, everything I had gleaned from every book I had read. As the mantle clock struck six, I realised I had no accommodation booked for the night and in voicing my predicament, the Professor invited me to his house on the outskirts of the city.

**MRS MAGUIRE**, housekeeper-cum-cook, gave me directions to my room. Dinner was at seven-thirty, so I unpacked my case, tested the bed and found it not wanting. Just before dinner I descended, finding myself eavesdropping:

"I'm not stopping and that's final. The rats in the cellar, amongst other things, have been clawing at the bottom of the door again. Leave the plates, I'll collect them up tomorrow. Good-night, Professor."

I continued down, pretending I had heard nothing. "Everything alright, Stephen?"

"Mrs Maguire had to leave – her sister is not at all well."

The lie intrigued me, but I merely smiled.

While we ate, the Professor talked of the African items in the house:

"Of course, there are still plenty of unpacked boxes in the cellar. I find that my time is better spent at the university than on my own private collection."

"What sort of items are down there?" I pressed.

"Difficult to tell . . . more wine?"

"Perhaps I could be of some assistance in cataloguing the items for you?"

"That would be very kind, but there is no

electric light – better if we look in the morning."

"But surly, it will be just as dark then as it is now?"

"Perhaps."

"Don't say that you are afraid – it's only a few rats at worst."

"You're right, of course, although on occasion I have detected a presence."

"I don't mind going on my own."

"No, I will come." He had just lit a paraffin lamp and unlocked the cellar door when the telephone rang; I took the lamp from him as he went back to answer the call. "Feel free to have a rummage while I'm gone."

The stone stairs were worn and the sulphurous yellow glow of the lamp made shadows dance to the swing of my stride. As I journeyed deeper, I discovered a haphazard heap of shields, spears, drums and carvings before my gaze fell upon an open trunk. My mind's eye perceived a dark disused sack slumped nearby, similar to a half-open umbrella, although as my light swept over it again, it's shape altered. I was sure it was no trick of the light, but persuaded my rational mind otherwise.

A black leathery hand uncurled, revealing long ragged talons. The thing shuffled towards me, its breath a dying gasp. The stench of rancid meat and excrement was overwhelming as it meat closed in on me. It stood less than half my height, though an extended arm grew longer than mine as it groped for purchase on my leg. I screamed, turning on my heels to run, the swinging lantern casting shadows to remind me of what lay behind. In sheer blind panic, I leapt up the stone steps but the hand clasped about my foot.

I screamed again as I was pulled relentlessly down. My left shoe suddenly slipped from my foot and I thrust myself up in desperation, twisting back around with the last of my strength, gaining first one step then another.

"Charles! What's the matter?"

I burst into the light, my legs finally buckling beneath me.

"Oh, you've lost your shoe – there it is, three steps down."

"Leave it, for God's sake, leave it."

"It's all right, I've got it."

I slammed the cellar door, locking it in one swift movement. Picking up my shoe I noticed there were five claw marks scored deep into the brown leather, leaving a trail of dark black lines. Then we both heard it – clawing, three times upon the bottom of the door.

"I am never free of it – it haunts me to my very soul. No matter how hard I try, I can't destroy it. For pity's sake, help me!"

"It came from Africa?"

The Professor nodded. "In the trunk that held the diary pages. I have them locked safe in my desk at the university," he whispered. "I thought it best they be kept as far from the trunk as possible. I had not the heart to destroy them."

"Would you mind if we fetch the pages now? I don't think I could sleep in this house anyway."

**WE ARRIVED** just as Millicent was shutting the door. One look from the Professor was enough for her to know that something was amiss.

"It's all right, Millicent," he said, but she came back inside the Professor's office, closing the door behind.

Unlocking his desk, he brought forth a folder. I pounced upon it with all the eagerness of a parched man on water, pulling the four pages free. They were burnt like the other six, but my eyes were immediately drawn to page two:

'– You are correct in thinking – never been able to get close enough – as you suggest, fire – you say it is Muti – African witchcraft – unable to destroy – distance may weaken – latching on – constant whisper – unable to sleep, but I have –'

Having had a taste of this thing I was already convinced that it must be destroyed, and I

voiced my opinion. The Professor had no option but to agree. We spent what remained of the night in the office having agreed to meet Millicent at the house the following morning, it being Mrs Maguire's day off.

**ON REACHING** the house, having picked up a stirrup pump from the porter's lodge, a small boy was unloading a hand cart containing several canisters of petrol; he left with a shilling for his trouble. Millicent was in the hall with a large tin bath, an African bow and several arrows. I put on a pair of wellington boots before starting our next task.

Once at the bottom of the cellar steps, the tin bath was loaded with the petrol canisters and stirrup pump. Millicent and the Professor tied strips of cloth behind the arrow heads while I dragged the tin bath into position. With trepidation, I emptied the petrol into the bath. Millicent dipped the arrows in the petrol then stood back as the Professor lit a candle, ready to pass the arrows when needed. I could see only cold defiance upon her face.

"Inverness ladies' archery champion, 1900," she said with determination.

I nodded, then pumped the petrol for all I was worth.

The bow twanged as Millicent's arrow hit the upturned lid of the trunk; a trail of burning light flew past me, engulfing the trunk in flames. A high-pitched scream came as the black shape shuffled towards me, already on fire. Snatching up one of the spears, it charged, bellowing a wail that shook me to my very core. I stumbled backwards and yelled, "For God's sake, get out!"

Millicent and the Professor made it to the steps but the thing was upon me, the spear taking a slice at my hip. I kicked over the tin bath, the petrol residue shooting upwards in a wall of flame. I ran as fast as my wound would

let me, the inhuman screams of the thing resounding in my ears. At the top of the steps, Millicent let her last arrow fly, striking home with a noise akin to a punctured wet blanket. The fabric of the thing burnt away, sending floating embers in all directions like some bizarre firework. With a curdling scream of vengeance, it hurled the assegai as I finally slammed the door shut, locking it in one swift motion.

**I AWOKE** in hospital, my side throbbing to remind me I was still alive.

"The doctor says you will live," Millicent informed me, as if there was a doubt that I might not.

"How long have I– "

"Two days – there was some type of poison on the spear tip. Luckily it had degraded over the years, or else you would not be with us now," the Professor said in a matter-of-fact way.

I raised myself up on my elbows. "Is it . . . gone?"

"Burnt to a crisp," Millicent shuddered. "Nothing left but some indistinct charred bones, but gone, yes."

*✑ ✑ ✑*

**I WENT** to convalesce at my brother's home in Kent, as far from Scotland as I could contrive. The Professor promised he would send on all I needed to complete my notes. I graciously accepted, although my ardour for all things African had somewhat abated.

At the beginning of November, a delivery arrived for me from Scotland; it contained two assegai spears, all the pages of the diary, and my brown shoes. A letter from Millicent and the Professor suggested I visit Scotland again soon, the place being all the less exciting without me.

Over the next few days my fascination with

Africa started to return and I worked steadily in the library. It was late evening on a Thursday when I became aware of a distinctive smell. The clean air entering the open windows cleansed the aroma, but the chill forced me to put a match to the fire. It was while I sat in the high-backed winged chair stoking the fire some thirty minutes later that I thought I heard my brother enter the room but, having my back to the door, I was unable to see him.

"I must thank you once again for such a pleasant evening. I can't remember when I–"

A rasping noise of slithering sack cloth returned the full horror of my nightmares; the stench was again overwhelming, the accompanying gasp like escaping steam. In blind panic, I shot out of the chair, spinning around with poker in hand, ready to confront the thing. But to my amazement, there was nothing, and in that

instant the smell was gone. I persuaded myself that I must have dozed off in front of the fire: waking with a start had broken the spell of my dream.

The next day I found that the library chair and the fire made me lethargic. Eventually, my eyes closed in blissful sleep. When I awoke, the fire had died down and, much to my surprise, my fob-watch said it was half-past four in the afternoon. The strange smell was back, although only mildly. I added some more coal to the fire and what was a meaningful step forward became a stumble back; the fire was scorching my legs, but I found I could not move.

The shape in the corner twitched in the firelight, moving towards me. I could distinctly hear shuffling, increasing to become the rhythmic smashing of shoe heels onto paving stone until my very brain resounded to their beat. Such was the pain it caused me that my nose began to bleed.

Somehow, I swung the poker, shocked, for the thing looked nothing like it had before; there was no outstretched clawed hand but instead a pair of feet, unbending at the knee but just as absurdly and frighteningly long. Clawed toes scratched into the floorboards as it scuttled like a pair of stilts towards me. The main body of the thing now more sack-like than sheet, but the stench was real enough for me.

With a gasping roar, it launched itself at me. Lashing out with the poker, I caught some of it, sending it spinning towards the fire. Within a heartbeat the thing was burning; the sackcloth combusting quickly in instant flames. A wailing scream stunned me: a sound that will always be with me. Within seconds it was out of the fire. The sudden advance knocked me off balance and we hit the floor. On top of me and then underneath me, the thing twisted and turned, all the while burning, and me along with it. I found I was screaming: "Die! Die! Die!"

The legs and clawed feet had raked gashing tears in my dress trousers; I could feel my blood feeding the thing even though it burned. The pain was excruciating as each lungful seared on the way down – I could feel blood in my throat. I was holding a shoe! – not just any shoe but a brown one; the maker's mark was all too clear for me to see. I was dying but my resolve was clear. With the last of my energy as we spun about the floor I threw the shoe into the fire; in an instant, the thing was lifeless. As I rolled away from it, the library door burst open.

"Charles . . . Charles! What the devil is– "

But I had already lost consciousness.

## THREE DAYS LATER: Alex and Sarah Baxter's house, Kent

I regret to have to tell you, dear reader, that my brother's time is near. Burns cover most of his body and his pain when breathing is beyond endurance, both for him and me, the listener of his rasping gasps. These brief entries have been penned by me, Alex James Baxter, dictated in the moments of my brother's lucidity. Charles is prescribed morphine for the pain but it does little for him. The doctors feel that moving him to hospital would kill him.

Charles Arthur Baxter died this day, November 13th, 1903.

His last words were: "Must destroy that which was touched."

## PRESENT DAY: Hallowe'en – October 31st, 1937.

I have compiled what I can, but sitting here in the house of my good friends, the Baxters – in the very library where Charles Baxter suffered such horrific injuries – does fill me with a great deal of apprehension. His final words leave me deeply perplexed, so I have been going through the diary pages again this afternoon.

The original text said: '– transfer of energy – latching on'.

In the last few moments, I could swear that an odour is seeping from the wall-mounted assegai, or perhaps it is just my imagination...

# AMONG OCTOBER'S FIELDS

## by Callum McKelvie

'DRAWN TO THE DARK', was how my mother used to describe me. No doubt it was this love for the 'darker' more unearthly aspects of life that drove me as I set off that night towards Riverbrook Home for Boys.

I had first heard whispers of the ruined orphanage whilst on a cycling holiday in Wiltshire. My morbid curiosity immediately hooked, I began to dig deeper. Research yielded very little at first. A few black and white pictures of young boys, a stunning photograph of a jovial woman with the most piercing eyes... and then the building itself. The stories came next. The tragic fire, all the children gone... and then the mysterious sounds across the fields at night.

I knew then I had found the inspiration I so desperately sought.

A brief correspondence with the local paper put me in touch with the caretaker, the aforementioned jovial woman and founder of the orphanage: Miss Cartwright. Finally, after months of deliberation, she consented to my visit but on two conditions. I was to come on October the 31st and to arrive at ten o'clock that same night.

So it was that at nine-thirty on October the 31st, I ventured across the fields towards Riverbrook. Soon the laughs and jeers of the public house where I had obtained a room faded into the distance and I was alone on my journey. However the night was a clear one and I felt no fear as I ventured further into that vast expanse of endless countryside. In the distance I could see a tiny light, no doubt indicating a small cottage where some aged farmer was occupied with warming himself by a roaring fire. I passed a small collection of carved pumpkins, but despite the jagged teeth and hollow eyes, the glow from their sinister grins was more comforting than horrifying on that cold, bitter night.

Soon however, I became aware of a singular change in atmosphere and, as I walked further, the fields that in the daylight had been so picturesque seemed vast and endless in the dark. Suddenly I found myself beset by the most intense loneliness. In the distance, vast mounds

of hay stood like huge, ancient monoliths. A solitary grand old oak watched me with quiet foreboding. Stripped of its leaves, I imagined how in the autumn sun it must have been beautiful in that decayed fashion that only October provides. Now it served only to remind me how alone I was. I passed the skeletal remains of a barn and its rotted timbers groaned disquietingly in the gentle breeze.

Then, rising up like the shadow of some vast colossus against the stars, I saw it.

Riverbrook.

The gutted, flame-ravaged ruin squatted amongst the grass. Two vast hollows where windows had once been stared out solemnly into the night.

Built onto a grand old farmhouse, the gothic monstrosity had an almost otherworldly feel amongst its setting of fields and crops. However, it was quite easy to see how, in its heyday, the building would have appealed to the enigmatic Miss Cartwright. Forgotten children of bustling smog-filled cities brought out to the country, amongst the endless fields and the smell of freshly-cut hay. There was certainly a romantic appeal to the concept. However, any romanticism that foreboding building had once held was gone and what remained resembled more the product of young boy's nightmare than his dreams.

Forcing my eyes away from the imposing structure, it was then that I became aware of the oddest of things. The ground surrounding the orphanage was littered with carved Jack-o'-lanterns. Nearing fifty of them. Indeed even further out towards fields I could see a faint glow indicating their presence. They varied somewhat in size and shape but one thing united them all…each wore the same sad, pitiful smile.

Indeed, such was the impression of utter and complete melancholy that I knew they were borne not of a child's fantasies.

Suddenly my thoughts were interrupted by the faintest of sounds behind me. Turning fast, I felt a feeling of the upmost horror possess me, as there, floating above the ground was one of the Jack-o'-lanterns.

'Mr Fanner?' A faint voice enquired with the soft lilt of an Irish accent.

The lantern lowered and I saw it was held in the hands of a tall spindly woman. Grey hair was bound in a bun and two piercing blue eyes stared emotionlessly out of sunken, ancient sockets. It was then that I realised I recognised the eyes. Yes! It was! Though I could scarcely believe it. Could this creature really be the same jovial woman as in the photograph? Could this really be Miss Cartwright?

'Mr Fanner I presume?' she asked again.

I gave a hurried nod, visibly attempting to regain the composure I had lost.

'I'm Miss Cartwright,' she responded.

I had hardly a moment to ponder the transformation before she, beckoning me to follow, led me to a small cottage just to the right of the orphanage.

However, I found myself unable to resist questioning the source of my momentary fright.

'These lanterns, why do you have them?' I asked

'Jack o' the lantern,' She responded curtly.

'I beg your pardon?' I said, trying to keep the bewilderment out of my voice.

'An Irish folk tale. He tricked the Devil so he couldn't take his soul, but his deceit barred him from the gates of Heaven. Forced to wander the Earth for all eternity, he carved a lantern and used it to find his way in the dark.'

'And that's why you carved them? To guide him and other spirits home?' I asked jovially.

'Oh I didn't carve them.'

And on that note she rushed ahead and into the cottage.

'I must ask again Mr Fanner, why it is you've come to Riverbrook?'

I had been staring at the rather imposing statue of the Virgin Mary, to the right of which Miss Cartwright had seated herself, when the stern voice pulled me from my thoughts. It was only one of a bizarre collection of items of both religious and folkish significance that decorated the interior of the cottage.

'As I explained in my letter Miss Cartwright,' I began, pausing to sup the rather excellent sherry which she had poured me, 'I am a writer, a writer in search of inspiration.'

'Yes, a ghost-story writer, I know some of your books,' she responded, making no attempt to hide her disdain at my craft.

Suddenly though those stern eyes fixed themselves upon me; 'But I am afraid that doesn't quite answer my question - why Riverbrook?'

'I'm…not quite sure I understand' I gulped the sherry, feeling somewhat uneasy in that bizarre little cottage.

She leant back, relaxing again and began to run her finger around the rim of her glass.

'Mr Fanner. Every town in England has a haunted house. On a lonely street in every village you'll find one. Where children tell tales of the whispers heard on the evening wind. Where floorboards creak in empty rooms. If inspiration is all you seek then I fail to see why Riverbrook alone should excite your imagination.'

'You're quite right of course, there are more houses like that than I could possibly visit,' I began, 'But I am a young man Miss Cartwright. My stories, though popular, they bore me so. The creaking floorboards, the attics with hidden secrets, they may intrigue my readers but they have driven me to desperation. Then… I found Riverbrook.'

'And you hoped that here you will find what you seek?'

She did not sigh, but the words were said with such complete and utter exhaustion that I swore a sigh I had heard.

I nodded.

For a moment the two of us sat staring at each other, when suddenly the old woman gulped down her sherry, threw her head back and let out a deep laugh.

'Oh Mr Fanner, you're a sweet boy, a little macabre perhaps, but sweet.' Then the laughing stopped. 'But I don't think you quite know what you've let yourself in for at Riverbrook – I think it best you leave now.'

'L-leave?!' I said astounded, but with raised hands the stern voice interrupted me.

'I've read your stories Mr Fanner. They're good, though as you say yourself a trifle romantic. I don't know quite know what you thought you'd find here. I thought that perhaps you might be able to help…help them understand, but I ask you now to turn and go. Go back to the city, back to where you came from before you find what you seek'.

There was no pause this time. Her words had seized me.

'Madam,' I began, 'In all my writing, all my reading, all my searching I've found only fantasy. You wish to know what I seek? I seek the truth. To know that there is more to my imaginings than idle fantasies.'

The pause again. My words had evidently struck some chord with the old woman. She thumbed the empty glass.

'You are sure?'

'Quite sure,' I responded firmly.

She looked into my eyes, then shaking her head in an obvious show of regret, consented. 'At the chime of eleven we go then, if you seek what you say, we must go only at eleven…'

For the next hour, we sipped our second glasses of sherry in silence.

We left precisely on the eleventh chime. Two oil lanterns our only companions. The autumn breeze had now turned to a bitter chill and the glow from the Jack-o'-lanterns cast perverse shadows across the path.

There, silent and waiting, *it* stood. Where the main entrance had once been there was now a pile of rubble. She took me to where the brickwork had collapsed enough to form a small

hollow at the side, a gaping cavern of darkness.

As we stood facing the mouth of that vast colossus, I was aware of a singular sense of the most intense dread. The old cliché of the shiver down the spine paled in comparison to the feeling that overtook me for that briefest of moments.

Then, led only by the light of the lantern, the spindly figure of Miss Cartwright disappeared inside.

If my host had noted my distress, she said nothing and I was compelled to follow.

As we headed towards the belly of the beast we passed a maze of rooms that I took to have been school rooms and dormitories. A tiny blackened object that might have once been a favourite toy, now left discarded in ash, crunched beneath my foot.

I noticed however, as we passed endless redbrick corridors, each scarred and blackened from the fire, that the damage seemed only to have occurred in isolated patches. Indeed it was hard to believe that the entire building had been ablaze, more that this was the work of short… concentrated blasts of flame.

We continued walking, the floor creaking precariously beneath my feet when my host asked:

'Do you know what the pagans called tonight Mr Fanner?'

The voice was as firm as ever and she never took her eyes off the light of the lantern.

'Samhain,' I responded, 'the festival of spirits.'

'Very good Mr Fanner, you really are a macabre boy.'

If humour had been intended, her tone did not indicate it.

'The day of spirits, when the doors to the otherworld were flung wide open. The hills ran red in the old country, anything to appease the gods. Do you know how the sacrifices were carried out?'

I shook my head and for the first time since we had entered that foreboding place, Miss

Cartwright took her eyes off the lantern and the two piercing orbs stared into my soul.

'They were burnt.'

I was given no chance to ponder my host's words before we entered on to an upstairs gallery and I saw the sinister spectre of the moon staring down from where the roof had collapsed. The most hellish of sounds filled my ear as charred and blackened beams creaked in the bitter wind.

We stood on a large central balcony overlooking what I took to have been the dining hall. Vast empty gaps, where windows had once been, gaped like hollow eyes whilst corridors jutted off as if they were tunnels in a labyrinth.

On the walls, white patches stood out. I admired the frames, whose rusted little nails had somehow survived the fire and clung on viciously. However valiantly they had once grasped, even they could not halt decades' worth of decay and had finally fallen from their places.

For a moment we stood in silence, then without warning, Miss Cartwright spoke: 'it seemed so ideal at first. The fields, the stream, the house. So peaceful, so perfect. Like a Constable painting.'

She wandered silently over to one of the gaping windows. Tiny dots of flame were visible in the distance. The jack-o'-lanterns. I thought of them there in the dark, with their sad smiles, and I shivered.

'The war was ravaging the continent then. The Great War. The raids, stories of invasion, those were dangerous times. The orphans... they were just left to fend for themselves. I wasn't wealthy, neither a figure of influence or respect. But I fought, by God I fought.'

She turned and cast her light about the room.

'And finally... I was able to secure these premises and the right to house refugees on them. I gathered a group of young idealists like myself and off we set. We had eight boys to begin with, but soon that number swelled to thirty.'

I felt my mouth hang open. I had been but a boy in the war too, though being British I had been a lucky one. I remembered the stories of the many little Belgian boys who hadn't been.

Yet here this woman was. A lone protector of the innocents, one who had fought so valiantly for their right to life. One couldn't help but feel admiration.

'And so you just moved down here? Without power or influence?!' I asked.

'Oh we were idealistic young things. We thought we could be self-sufficient, set up a farm on the grounds. Teach the boys to work the land. We built the barns, bought the machinery, indeed I think we would have been successful had we not made one fatal mistake. Our choice of farmhand. Our choice of Slatter.'

As she said the name I had the faintest notion that I saw the light of the jack-o'-lanterns flicker in the distance, but I put it from my mind.

'He came here with his father. Eighteen, tall and lanky...but the strangest face. Thin, pock-marked with hollow cheeks and eyes like two-lumps of black coal.'

She paced towards the balcony, looking down on the empty hall below.

'His father scarcely let us see him. Never spoke or mentioned the boy unless he had to. At dinner the teen would sit in silence. It was a year before I heard a word out of him. The other girls used to call him 'strange'...aye he was that. I used to see him in the fields sometimes...talking...with no one there.'

The spindly figure moved back towards the window, her eyes fixed on the barn I had passed earlier.

'But talented. That boy could work the land like no one I had ever seen. Those crooked little fingers could plant anything and it would grow. But the boy's father wouldn't leave him in the fields alone. It took me some time to realise why he didn't speak of him.'

Miss Cartwright turned stiffly, the light catching the wetness beginning to form in her eyes and with a shaking voice she said:

'He was afraid of him.'

As quickly as she had turned she was back facing out again. Her voice was still and calm as she continued.

'Then, a few months later... the boy's father was dead. There had been an accident with the scythe. No witnesses. I was all prepared to hire

another hand but the boy... how he sobbed, sobbed and begged. He had nothing else in the world but his father, his father and the farm.'

She let out a long sigh, leaning back against the window frame.

'And so I was a fool. I let him stay. But is it so foolish if one is blinded not by greed or selfishness, but by pity?'

She sighed again, her eyes moving once more to the jack-o'-lanterns, and for the first time that evening I felt overcome by a feeling of immense guilt. The strain that recounting these obviously painful events was taking on her was visible.

I began to realise why it was impossible to romanticise Riverbrook.

'To begin, the effect was positive... the children loved him, he taught them games, took them for walks across the fields...then it started.'

As she spoke, I checked my watch. Twenty-to-midnight.

'Little things at first. One or two of the boys misbehaving, scaring the others with stories of a goblin in the fields. Then, it got worse...we found them wandering the crops at night. Slatter became distant. He wouldn't let anyone in the barn. I used to hear him in the early hours of the morning, chanting and when I knocked he didn't answer. There was something else too...in the air.'

She turned and was facing me again.

'Not just the boys Mr Fanner. The land. It bloomed. It bloomed during harvest, when no

crops had been laid...then in October....it got worse.'

I could almost hear the cogs whirring within my own mind.

'Near Samhain?' I asked.

She simply nodded a response: 'Then that evening. The unthinkable happened. The boys went missing. At nine we found them, wandering the fields...marks on their backs like claws.'

She paused, swallowed deeply and composed herself.

'They would not speak of what had happened.'

I felt a sickness rise in my throat and a sudden queasiness that forced me to grip onto the brittle bannister. After a moment, I was able to compose myself.

'I tried to phone the police, but the lines...they'd been cut. I was resolved to take the boys as far away as possible if I could. We spent the night packing...when it started.'

She stared out at the ruin of the barn.

'Noises...like none you've ever heard, chanting too, all of them coming from the barn. Then: flashes, strange lights...the very fields themselves seemed to roar as if something was coming.'

'S-something?' I didn't mean to stutter.

My question was ignored: 'Earlier I asked you about Samhain. Do you know what the purest sacrifice was Mr Fanner?'

I shook my head, though I think inside I knew the answer.

'A child.'

The nauseous feeling returned.

'The boys were hysterical, my staff too. I couldn't take it. I wanted to run–'

Her pale hand gripped the stone window frame.

'But then I noticed one of the boys was missing. Somehow, I don't quite know how, I knew Slatter was at the centre. I had to do *something*.'

She paused now. The shaking in her voice had returned.

'The barn itself seemed to glow with a deep crimson unlike any fire I'd ever seen. The noise was deafening... but still, I went to open the door.'

I glanced frightfully at my watch. Midnight.

'Slatter was in the centre of the room. Chanting. Naked... but he wasn't alone... *it* was there.'

'I-it?' I cursed my own cowardice as the second stammer escaped me.

Miss Cartwright didn't take her eyes off the fields.

'I didn't get a good look...it was tall, spindly but muscular. Like a spider that had suddenly learnt to walk on two legs. Its skin...it looked like fallen leaves, brown and dry as one often finds in autumn...no it was dried leaves and hay too, compacted and encrusted with mud...I was only able to make out a perverse grin of crooked jagged teeth...when...'

She gave a sharp intake of breath, her eyes staring blankly as if the thing was still there in front of her.

'Whatever it was, it noticed me. Slatter gave a cry of panic, but then the thing spat a ball of flame and Slatter seemed to *ignite*. I was able to catch one last look at the thing, racing towards the house before me - I...I...'

She didn't look at me.

'I fainted.'

I cursed my curiosity. Cursed it for driving me forward even now. But I had to know.

'W-what did it look like?'

And turning, those sad wet eyes looking directly at me, Miss Cartwright responded:

'It had a face I'd seen before. A face I'd seen since I was a child...it had the face of a jack-o'-lantern.'

Then, at that precise moment, there was a distinct gust of wind that rattled the very foundations of the ruined orphanage.

To this day I swear that, in that same wind, I heard the sounds of a young boy's sobs.

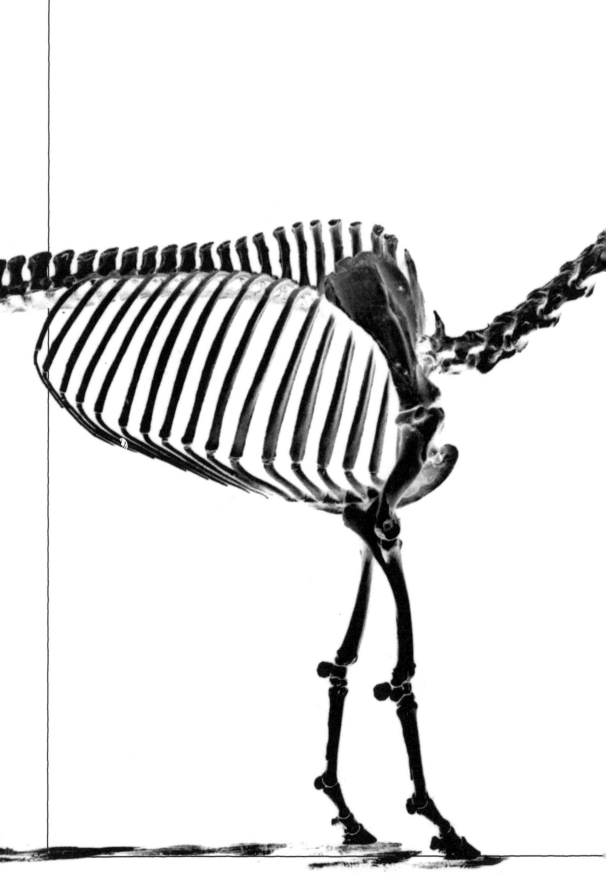

# IN WE COME

## ❧ ❧ ❧ by Alys Hobbs ❧ ❧ ❧

**ONE NIGHT** at the end of October, my parents went out and left me alone.

There was a party for them to go to. A grown-up dinner. Friends I didn't know. "You'd only be bored, darling," my mother said, spritzing perfume and filling the bathroom with roses. Father smacked on aftershave, fastened cufflinks, poured himself a scotch. "Go to bed early," he said. "Stay out of the fridge. Don't stay up watching television."

I sat on the staircase and watched them leave. Watched them distort behind the frosted glass window, watched their shadows stretch away along the front path. After a minute I got up and flung the door open, wanting to run after them and beg them to take me along. But they were gone. Not even their voices carried back down the lane.

I stood for a moment and stared out into the dark. We were the last house in town, right on the edge of the moors. There were no streetlights out here, no comforting glows from nearby neighbours. No cars passing. Not even a moon.

A flurry of wind ran through the hedgerow. I shut the door and retreated to my seat on the stairs. The house felt still, so silent I could hear the carriage clock on the living room mantelpiece as though it was right next to my ear.

Tick. Tick.

I jumped up. I darted from room to room turning on all the lights. I switched on the television and flicked through the channels. A talk show. A news report. A documentary. A silent film about weeping nuns. Every one of them flickering and crackling; the wind on the lines, my father always said. I chose the talk show and turned the volume up.

When I heard the front door open, I almost jumped out of my skin. I hadn't expected my parents back so early, but here they were – about to catch me staying up, watching television, doing what they'd told me not to.

But it wasn't my mother who walked in. It wasn't my father.

He was so tall, the man who came into the sitting room, that he had to duck his head under the doorframe. He was dressed in a smock that might once have been white, a butcher's apron strained across his round belly. Over his head, an old sack. Two eyeholes cut out. A slash for a red nose to peek out of. Crudely drawn lips where the mouth should have been. And in his hands, a cleaving knife.

I sat frozen, my mind groping for explanations, finding nothing. Too large, too grubby and grotesque in the familiar blandness of my house, the butcher seemed to fill the room. Carriage clock. Cream carpet. Sofa covers. Family photos. Then the butcher, a gaping hole stabbed through reality, leering out, towering over.

He took one big exaggerated step into the room, then stopped, starting at me. Silent, as though waiting for me to speak first. My blood was hammering in my ears – this was a trick, a joke. He was lost. On his way to a party. I would tell him that my parents weren't here. That he had the wrong house. Then he'd leave.

I opened my mouth to speak.

Then a voice burst from the butcher, knocking me speechless again. A voice like a horn, nasal and booming.

"Make room!" he blared, and he bent his knee and swept his cleaving knife in a wide circle, as though clearing a space among many people. The knife flopped as he swung it. I realised it was made of cardboard and tin-foil.

"Make room, for in we come!"

He spun around, his arms spread wide, and came to face me again.

"We've come a-mumming," he said. "Three-two-one!"

Mumming. I knew that word. I realised what was happening. Or I thought I did.

My parents had told me about the local tradition, although my mother said no-one did it any more. It was some kind of folk custom – a thing from the old days, when people had nothing better to do.

On Halloween night, a group of people would dress up in masks and roam the dark streets of the village. They would come into your house, uninvited, and they would put on a play. If you wanted them to leave, you had to give them money or food. Even though they were in disguise, everyone knew – or thought they knew – who they were under the masks. It was all a bit of a joke, according to my father. But my mother insisted there was something in it – that not playing along could tempt fate. That turning the mummers away could welcome something worse in. Whether it was true or not, it was only a game. Some of the locals must have decided to start it up again. And now that I knew what was going on, I found I could move. I sat up, intending again to say that my

parents were out, so the man should come back later – although I hoped he wouldn't.

"My–"

"We hope you'll be kind?" the butcher interrupted, wagging his finger, leaning down toward me. "That you will not complain? Obey and you won't see us back here again!"

I caught a reek from him then; a real smell of meat, sickly-sweet, a flowery powder tinge.

"My mum and dad are out," I said. My voice sounded strange to my own ears, so trembling and faint. "You could–"

The front door banged open again. I whirled around, straining to see my parents come in arm in arm. They would walk in, see the mummer, and their faces would light up at the novelty of it all. They would laugh. Play along. It would all be fine.

But my heart lurched. The thing that crept in was not my parents, and it was far worse than the butcher.

A skeletal horse, daubed in red paint, its body one great hump covered in a scarlet sheet. It lumbered into the room in a slow, loping motion, knocking an ornament off the side table, which cracked in half.

The horse head swung to-and-fro. Looking around. To and fro.

The butcher stepped back with a sweeping bow. He gave the horse centre stage.

"Here I am," said the horse. Its voice was a rattle, a dry crackling dead-leaf rasp. "Here I am. Watch me close. Watch my trick."

The horse head jittered, and I saw that its neck was a wooden stick. My fear eased again; not a real skeleton, of course. There was a person under there, only a stupid person, bent over, holding up the skull of a dead horse on an old broom handle.

"You know me, sweet watchers!" it said. Clearly these people had a script that they were going to stick to, no matter who was in the room. The horse skull swooped closer to me. It lowered its voice to a pantomime whisper, confiding a secret for the whole room to hear. "You can call me – Old Nick!"

And the horse began to caper. It jumped up in the air, its skull knocking against the lampshade, making the light swing, casting mad black shadows around the room. As it pranced it neighed and screeched. The butcher cowered, averting his eyes. I sat clutching the

arms of my chair. Even though I knew it was a person under that sheet, the sight still filled with me with a sick, queasy feeling. A feeling that something was very wrong; that something had changed in my house, in my life, that something had been taken, or spoiled, and could never be put back to how it was.

As the horse pranced, it finished its lines. "I've disguised myself cleverly – as this ragged old nag – to roam here on earth with yonder young slag!"

My cheeks flushed. The swear word had caught me off guard. The horse and the butcher both stopped moving at once, and they swung their heads toward the hallway.

And it shouldn't have been horrible, the thing that

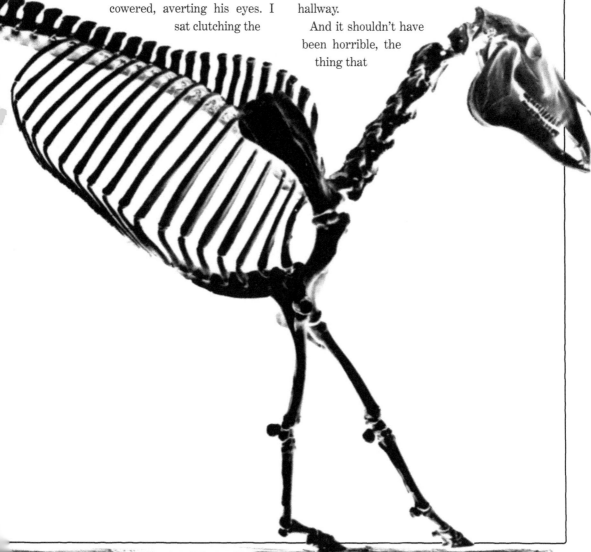

came in next. It should even have been funny. A man dressed as a woman – or something like a woman. Her face made of odd patches of putty-like, fleshy material, all shaded in pinks and purples. Her mouth lipstick-smeared, her false eyelashes so long they curled right up to her forehead. Her bosom was foam, moulded into two huge breasts that spilled out from an old-fashioned smock. She staggered on high heels, the ringlets of her blonde wig rolling across her back. And as she came in she simpered, made high cooing sounds in mockery of a woman's voice. She went to the horse. Draped her arms around it.

"Oh, look!" she cried, "Look at him. My sweet, handsome steed! As black as the treacle! As tall as a weed!"

The butcher, now watching on his knees, clasped his hands to his sack face as though sharing in her delight. He motioned to me that I should do the same. My hands twitched. I tried to shake my head at him, to tell him I didn't want to join in, I didn't want to play.

The way the woman embraced the horse made my gut twist; it was not the way a woman would usually behave with an animal.

"Oh, how I love him!" she moaned, turning her horrible face to where I sat. Her eyelashes cast her eyes into shadow, but I still thought she tried not to look straight at me. "But–" she sighed, stepping back from the horse and turning out her pockets to show they were empty, "I have nothing left." She pressed the back of her hand to her forehead in despair. "I must sell my sweet horse, or else I'll starve to death!"

There was a pause here, all three actors frozen in their stance. The woman in her dismay, the horse preening, the butcher on his knees looking on. I got the impression that they were waiting for a reaction from the audience – from me.

I swallowed a great lump in my throat.

Again, I whispered, "my mum and–"

"I am the butcher!" Once more the butcher's voice barged across my own. He tottered to his feet, his round belly lurching to one side. I realised that his stomach, too, was made of foam. He was wearing short wooden stilts to make himself taller.

"Young lass, if you're willing – I'll buy that nag off you, and pay you a shilling!" From his dirty apron the butcher produced a big, fake coin. He pressed it into the woman's hand. She drew a deep breath, but he pressed a finger to her lips. "No!" he said, "don't say a word, my dear! Don't try to speak! He'll be feeding a family of four for a week!"

The woman staggered back. The horse tried to lurch away. But the butcher seized it by the scruff of its neck, and he swung his cardboard cleaver into the beast's stomach.

The horse made a terrible noise, a strangled scream far more convincing than anything that had come before. It flung itself to the floor. I saw a motion under the red sheet, as though hands beneath were groping. Then it lay still.

The butcher stood triumphant, and the woman threw herself upon the horse's body, sobbing. She wailed for what seemed a long time - so long that I wondered if someone else had forgotten their lines. The carriage clock ticked. She howled. She moaned. She d r a g g e d her fingers over the horse's back. The butcher waited, rocking on his stilts, until finally the woman reared her head again.

"My beauty!" she screamed, her voice tearing with an anguish that seemed very real. "My treasure!" and she flashed out her hand to me like a cobra striking. "Sweet watcher," she said, "I pray! Take up your part – play our doctor today!"

I gaped. I stammered. I shook my head, recoiled, did everything a child does when he doesn't want to be pulled onto the stage. But the woman stretched her arm out

urging me on. Give him life. They went on and on, past any point of comedy or theatre, until it became clear that they were not going to give up until I did what they said.

So I slid from the armchair, my legs aching from how long I had sat tensed-up, my shirt stuck to my back with cold sweat.

They rolled the horse over onto its back. Its long, white, beak-like nose pointed up at the ceiling. They indicated that I should put my

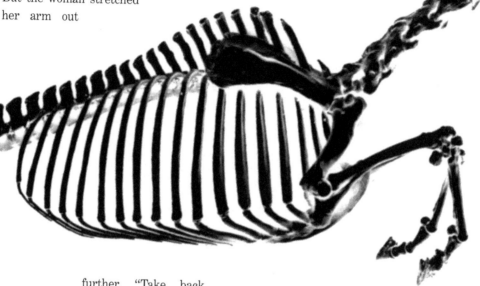

further. "Take back what the butcher has done with his knife!" she implored. "Won't you lend me your hand, and give my love life?"

And then she and the butcher began to speak at the same time, their voices low and soft – give him life, they chanted. Give him life. Give him life.

I kept on shaking my head. I tried to tell them I wasn't allowed, they had to leave, my parents would be back any minute. But they paid me no attention. They kept on chanting. Give him life, they said. Give him life. The woman's hand still outstretched. The butcher nodding his head hugely with every repetition,

hands onto the horse's chest. I guessed that in the realm of this awful play, that would be enough to heal the creature. Then we would go on to some happy finale. And it would all be over.

Give him life. Give him life. Their voices droned in my ears, filling my exhausted brain with an insect hum. I had no choice. I pressed my trembling hands to the spot on the sheet that they pointed to.

I expected to feel something solid beneath. The real, human bulk of a body beneath the costume. But my hands pressed in, and pressed in, into softness, into horrible damp warmth, into emptiness. I watched my arms sink in up to the wrist, and in, touching nothing. The scarlet sheet like liquid, fluid and soft under my palms, and never giving way. I felt I could have pushed forever, up to my elbows, up to my shoulders, plunging on, and on, and down into that endless red, wet heat.

Then beneath my hand, something pushed back.

With a strangled scream I yanked backwards. I staggered up onto my feet, catching my legs, falling back into the armchair, gasping for breath.

The horse stood up from the floor. It did so without theatrics; simply stood, its long skull lifted from its chest. But something had changed. The damp, horrible heat seemed to have leaked out of the horse, into the air. The room seemed smaller, the light sick and yellow, the shadows deeper. The smell of meat stronger than ever, raw and sticky, coating my throat.

I felt like I needed to run. But I couldn't move. And after what felt like an hour, the woman and the butcher stood too. Whatever had happened, now the ending would come. A conclusion. The big reveal. I would grab some money from the emergency jar, they would leave, laughing, joking, human. Actors after a performance.

But none of the mummers spoke. One by one, they turned and walked from the room. There were no final speeches. They didn't even take a bow. The horse strode away, moving like a fish downstream, its red sheet billowing. Then the woman followed, her arms limp at her sides. Then the butcher, tottering on his stilts. They went to the hall, through the front door, down the garden path. Out onto the lane. Into the dark. Gone.

I sat for a few long minutes, trembling, my cheeks damp with sweat or tears. Then I wrenched myself out of the chair, flung myself to the front door and slammed it shut. Locked it. I tumbled up the stairs and into my room, to my bed. I burrowed beneath the covers. And I lay there among my heavy breath, staring straight ahead, clenching my hands which shook and spasmed. That wet heat still clung.

Some time later, my parents returned home. They seemed in good spirits, giggling together as they came up the stairs. And I'm not sure why I didn't tell them about what had happened. Perhaps I thought they wouldn't believe me. For some reason I thought they might have even been angry. But I told them I wasn't feeling well. I took the blame for breaking the ornament in the living room. My mother kissed me, my father turned off the light. I listened to them getting ready for bed, to their comfortable chatter, gradually falling to silence, the house becoming still again.

My room felt strange; both hot and cold, and as though things were not quite in their right places. Sleepless hours passed. I heard the chime of the clock downstairs. Midnight. One. Two. Three.

I sat up. Got out of bed. Went to the window. It was like someone had called me from outside, and that I had no choice but to go.

That window looked out over the moors; over miles of bleak landscape, acres of grey stone. Over wild grass and still pools and deep, lonely marshland where mindless things crept and slithered in the ditches. On this night in October, with the end of the year on its way, the darkness was absolute. Only the wind was moving, bending the bare arms of the trees, wandering through the long weeds.

And far off in the blackness, a fire burned.

SAMHAIN — LEONA PRESTON

# HOW SHADOWS FALL
## *by* C. L. Hanlon

LONELY stretch of motorway, the colour of dull metal, miles before it reaches the city. Rusting barbed wire and oily poisoned grass. Industrial units and brand new, empty office buildings. Chemical factories and long abandoned mills. No one ever stops here. There is nothing to stop for. Cars and lorries thunder on and on, into the north. It only quietens at 3 a.m., lit by rearing sentinels of lights. Sometimes shadows move, beneath the concrete bridges, but there is no one to see them.

Gina walks quickly along the hard shoulder. She's cold, in her summer dress and sandals, and she wraps her arms around herself, head bent as she hurries along. It will be getting dark soon. The sun is going down behind the chemical factories in a blaze of toxic orange. She must get back to the car. Ryan was angry with her, but he's had time to calm down. It should be ok now. A container lorry blasts past her, with a gust of wind, smelling of metal and petrol fumes, makes her stagger. She hurries on, conscious of the distance she has yet to cover, and the approaching darkness.

Alan is tired. He feels as if he's been driving forever and his eyes are itching with exhaustion. He takes another toffee from the glove box, with one weary eye on the huge lorries that grind past him. He knows he should stop and rest, but there is nowhere around here to stop. Huge, empty, plate glass and metal office blocks bearing TO LET signs and the desolate sprawl of the chemical factories. Far above him the carriageway lights are coming on. He feels the last of the day slipping away from him and drives on.

Gina is colder now. She clutches her chilled arms tightly and tries to walk faster, but her legs are aching with cold and fatigue. The sun has slipped beneath the horizon and light is draining from the sky. She pictures Ryan standing by the car and her eyes prickle with tears of self-pity. She seems to have been walking for miles yet there is nothing ahead of her but more motorway, and the abandoned factories where grey shadows are lengthening. She does not want to be alone out here in the

dark. She rubs at the bruises on her arms and looks uneasily around her. Something flickers at the very edge of her vision. A shadow? A person? Surprise and fear make her come to an abrupt halt. A human figure is standing just beyond a doorway in the decaying factory. With the last of the light behind it, she can't make out any features, but it seems to be looking in her direction. She stands, looking back. Should she wave? Shout for help? Another lorry thunders past, a gust of warm, gritty air in its wake. The figure doesn't move. It stands, arms at its sides, its blank face looking at her. Gina looks away and walks on quickly. Someone sleeping rough, a tramp, a junkie, is not going to be able to help her.

It gets darker and colder. Drifts of rain blow across the motorway and Alan switches on the windscreen wipers. He knows that it's pointless to go on driving and searching after dark, but something makes him press on. He puts the radio on but all he gets is a blast of static and a woman's voice fading in and out. Just another hour, he tells himself, and he'll call it a day and give up.

The rain is fine but chilly, soaking Gina's thin dress quickly. There is another flicker from the corner of her eye and she jerks her head around to see a second figure emerging from the shadowed factory. It seems to see her and stops abruptly, arms hanging limp at its sides, gazing in her direction. Gina's pace stutters and she trips in her sodden sandals. More figures are coming forwards from the darkness of the factory yard. They form a ragged line under the darkening sky, not acknowledging her in any way, though she has no doubt they are staring at her. Fear makes her run, clumsily, blundering to the next pool of weak yellow light. Her breath rasps in her throat and she can hear herself sobbing. She waves at the cars and lorries streaming heedlessly past her. Their drivers wear grey, fixed expressions, they don't see her. She stumbles on, convinced she can feel the strange figures keeping pace with her on the rubbish strewn embankment. A concrete bridge ahead offers a kind of sanctuary. She huddles beneath it, taking deep, shuddering breaths. The traffic swishes past her, on its way to somewhere else. She is alone out here in this terrible place.

Alan sees her cowering beneath the bridge. A little drowned rat of a girl, alone and terrified. At the last minute he slows and pulls over.

"Are you ok?"

Gina looks at him warily. Can he be trusted? He'll have to be, if she's going to get away from here. He opens the car door.

"Come on, I'll take you to the next services. Are you lost?"

Gina's trembling legs take her over to the car and she climbs in. The warmth makes her gasp and shiver. He reaches into the back seat and hands her a tartan blanket. It's like the one her dad used to keep in his car. He looks a bit like her dad, too. Solid and dependable. He smiles at her as he steers back into the traffic.

"Better?"

Gina nods. "Yes. Yes, thank you. The car broke down. I went to phone and..." She lets the words trail off. She doesn't want to mention Ryan, or Ryan's temper, or the fact that it was her who'd forgotten to put fuel in the car, so Ryan was right when he said she had to walk to the emergency phone. She sees the man glancing at her bruised wrist and quickly slides it beneath the blanket.

"Is it far? I've been walking for ages. And I couldn't find the car, and then I saw…I thought I saw…' Once more, she can't finish. Alan shakes his head.

"Not safe out here at night. You don't know who's about. I'm picking up my daughter. I wouldn't let her walk along here by herself in the daytime, let alone at this time."

Gina glances at him. The warmth and feeling of safety are relaxing her gradually. The windscreen wipers swish and cluck reassuringly. She huddles into the seat and weariness makes her eyelids heavy. It seems only a moment until she opens her eyes again, and she sees the road is empty ahead of them. The rain has stopped, and clouds of mist are drifting across the carriageway.

"Here we are, lass." Alan slows the car and pulls over. Gina throws off the blanket and looks around her.

"Is this the services? Where are we?" She can't see any lights or any other cars. Just the ribbon of motorway stretching ahead of them into the darkness. She looks at Alan, but he is staring straight in front of him.

"You'll be fine now," he says.

"But this isn't…" Gina starts, then something about his fixed gaze stops her. She opens the door and gets out. They have stopped beside one of the huge giraffe-necked lights. There are bunches of flowers tied to it, and a card, ink running in the rain. She steps closer to read it. "Darling husband and daughter…taken from me…your heartbroken mum and wife." Gina pushes her wet hair back from her face and turns to Alan. "Is this…?"

She is alone on the wet road. No car. No Alan. The motorway is utterly quiet and empty. She turns in a circle, fear and confusion rising. He was here. He was real. Except he wasn't. Only drifts of fog and a watery semi-circle of moon in the night sky. Gina scrambles up the wet embankment, thinking she will see the tail lights of a car speeding into the distance. But there is nothing, the motorway is empty for miles. She turns the other way, and sees across a field the lights of a service station. Warmth and safety. People. A phone. She climbs the fence and begins to walk.

# ᕦhe TEMPLE
## by Florence Vincent

BY 8 A.M. the temperature had topped thirty, and the air had begun to cling to her skin like a wet woollen dress. Olivia rearranged the shawl on her shoulders, seeking an inlet of air, wishing she could tear it off altogether. With a little fussing she found that if she walked with her arms stuck out, hands on her hipbones, a slight breeze would slink through her armpits.

Claire was pushing through the crowds to jostle for the good photo-taking spots. Olivia finally found her crouched by the lake, taking shots of the temple and the clear lines of its still reflection. Flies skittered across the surface of the water, and there was a hum of voices and cicadas. A woman in a long red dress stood on the opposite bank from Claire seeming to look over at her, or perhaps at the trees beyond, and there – Olivia sheltered her eyes with her hand – sitting on a little run of broken down wall, was a monkey inspecting its genitals. Olivia thought of calling out to Claire but just stood letting her mouth hang open for a moment. She moved her eyes to the back of Claire's heel, where she could see the clean white square of bandage, and thought of the night before, the way the blister oozed blood as Claire slid a needle into its heart. *I don't know why you're so squeamish*, she said, shrugging her shoulders in the same way she had this morning, when Olivia held her stomach and said she didn't think she was well enough to go.

After the crowds started to disperse, Olivia and Claire trailed inside. They walked slowly, not talking, first through the outer walls of the complex, and then into the inner ring. Though she didn't say it, Olivia felt there was something unpleasant in the emptiness of the corridors, the way they seemed to go nowhere, the way the shadows moved constantly, painting the walls in shifting stripes of brown and gold. At the end of one corridor they came upon a shrine and a man thrust incense sticks into their hands. After Claire had lit hers, the man demanded money and Olivia felt a familiar feeling of clamping, pointless embarrassment, and had to turn her face to the ground.

"You should have done one with me," said Claire afterwards. "Why do you always leave these things to me?"

Olivia was still thinking of something to say when Claire turned and walked off down the corridor. Eventually Olivia went to find her, but there was no sign of her, no flash of orange head wrap or the turquoise batik shawl she had haggled for on the Khao San Road. Olivia wanted suddenly to hold the shawl in her hands, to put it to her face and smell its spicy human scent. She walked back the way she came, past the shrine, tipping a handful of coins into the man's palm as she went. Then, turning left when she had meant to turn right, through a doorway she hadn't seen before, she collided with someone.

"I'm so sorry," she said, helping the person to their feet, and seeing that it was the woman in the long red dress. "Did I hurt you?" The other woman raised an arm and pointed towards the doorway ahead, from which she must have just come. Her dress was wet, as though she had just walked in from the rain.

"She's in there."

The woman went outside again, a corner of her soaked dress catching, just for a moment, on Olivia's trousers. The woman had seen her and Claire together earlier at the lake. She was trying to be helpful. Olivia said this to herself, trying to shake off the feeling of oddness that had come down over her.

She peered into the doorway, which opened on to a set of stairs moving downwards. At the bottom, a wash of cheerful gold sun was coming across the lower wall. The sight of it made her feel better, and so she started down, coming out into an enclosed area, lidded with a square of flat blue sky. Four high walls slanted upwards from a walkway surrounding an empty square enclosure. From the looks of it, the door Olivia had come from was the only entrance. Casting her eyes around, she found no sign of Claire. She peered into the enclosure in the centre and found it wasn't empty. At the bottom, far below, was a pool of green water, off which was rising a faint stagnant smell. Olivia sniffed the air, finding another odour behind it, something she couldn't quite put her finger on, something dimly tapping at an old memory.

A fleeting feeling of dread came across her and she let it pass. It wasn't an area intended for visitors, she decided. She must have gotten through accidentally; perhaps the woman in red had opened it and she had mistakenly wandered inside. She decided now she was here that she would follow the length of the walkway, take some pictures to show Claire as a record of her solo adventure.

Turning to the right, Olivia began to walk, putting out a palm and drawing it along the stone as she went. She hadn't noticed it at first but the air in here was cooler. She cast a look behind her and slipped the shawl off her shoulders and let out a little cackle, rounding the first corner and then the second and coming up to the opposite side of the square. It was at this point that she heard Claire's voice. Turning, she saw a corner of turquoise shawl, a square of white bandage disappear into the dark doorway opposite.

"Claire!" she called out, quickly retracing her steps to the entrance. She must have been hiding. It was a little game, all was forgiven. Relief flooded through her; it was like they were already back at the hotel, swimming in the big cold pool, lying on the bed with the fan on, legs twined together. Olivia rounded the last corner and looked ahead, readying herself to dart into the dark entrance. But now, strangely, she seemed unable to see it.

She blinked, took a step back and looked again, casting her eyes across the full span of the wall. It seemed entirely solid. Strange, she thought, that she could have gotten so turned around. Turning and looking back at the wall opposite, her breath caught in her throat. A flash of turquoise scarf, a bandaged heel, were disappearing into the darkness of an entranceway that hadn't existed moments before.

"This heat! It's getting to me," she said out loud for comfort, finding her voice thin and strange. She forced a laugh, feeling something uncoiling in her stomach, and began to head in

the direction of the doorway, keeping her eyes on it. As she walked she smelt the smell of the green lake below. It was an odour of stagnant water, yes, but also something else she couldn't place. What was it? An edge of burning, and something acidic, like bleach or strong vinegar. She stopped and peered down. The water appeared higher than before. Something on the surface seemed to ripple. She stepped back, looked up at the black doorway she had fixed her eyes on moments before, the doorway Claire had disappeared into, and found it wasn't there.

"Claire," she heard herself say. "Where are you?" and tried to force a laugh that wouldn't come. She looked at the wall behind her, the wall to her left, and the wall to her right, and finally ahead at the span of bricks opposite, where – how? – she could see, just disappearing into the dark rectangle of a doorway, a triangle of turquoise scarf, a foot with a white bandage.

"Claire," she called out, hearing no sound. She ran towards the door, kicking up dust, not taking her eyes from the black rectangle. And as she grew closer she could smell it, the smell of Claire's scarf, the human, true smell of the skin-warm fabric. But there was another smell behind it, a burning smell, a smell of old lake water, and of bleach, and of vomit. It was strong now, so strong she couldn't help but turn her head to look down. The green lake water was lapping at the edges of its recess, inches from her feet, the surface of it shifting like hands underneath a blanket. Staring down at it Olivia at last felt the memory come back. She was reminded of the smell of the family cat, gone missing for two weeks and finally discovered in a corner of the attic, the fur peeling back and the black insides shivering with maggots.

*Claire*, Olivia mouthed and stepped backwards, putting her hand out for a doorway that wasn't there anymore.

# F O G T I M E
## by Catrin Kean
### Illustrations by M.S. CORLEY

I CAN REMEMBER THE NIGHT I was born.

I'm thinking about it because it's my birthday and I'm going down the hill to get chips for Mammy and me. I know she's thinking about it too because as soon as the fogtime comes she locks the doors and windows and pulls all the curtains across and turns the telly up too loud.

The night I was born there was a sweet sulphur-scented wind blowing through the window and white curtains flying, and outside the sparkly town was all blurred in the mist. Down the hill dragon-tongued flames from the furnaces licked at the sky. I looked up at Mammy who was all pink-cheeked and pretty, and Daddy who was kissing her salty hair. They were happy.

The windows of the pub on the corner are decorated with spider-webs and someone's singing 'Midnight Train To Georgia' on the karaoke, all out of tune and shouty. An old woman sits outside wrapped in a man's woollen coat, caught in a wreath of webbed light. She's smoking a roll-up and as I walk past she spits tobacco at the ground.

The town's lit up with burning pumpkins. Fire-faces grin from windows and children in bedsheets run from door to door swinging rattling buckets. There's music shimmying up the hill from the main street. There are shadowy figures in the alleys, lights dancing from their fags and phones like fireflies. The hooded boys fall silent as monks as I pass though the light at the end of the alley, and the girls move closer together and laugh loudly at an invented joke, pretending not to see me. If the girls weren't there the boys would follow me, keeping to the shadows like cats, wanting to but not daring to come near.

Except the time one of them was braver.

After I was born they said Mammy'd gone

mad and they took us away to live in a mental hospital for a year. I think that's why my hair is grey though people say silver when they're trying to be nice. After the mental hospital we came back home and Daddy was gone and Mammy never smiled any more.

They've decorated the board outside the chip shop like a gravestone and it says 'COME IN IF YOU DARE. SCARILY GOOD FISH AND CHIPS' which I think is funny. The shop is decorated inside with little strings of lights with ghost faces on and the staff are wearing witches' hats. I ask for two fish and chips, large, with mushy peas, and because it's my birthday I add a saveloy for Mammy and a pineapple fritter for me. Salt and vinegar, yes please. The boy who serves me doesn't look at me because he feels stupid in his hat but when he gives me my change his fingers touch my palm. This is the boy who was brave. I walk back up the hill with an armful of warm chips wrapped in paper. There's the sound of rat-a-tatting on doors and silhouettes of children darting through the fog. The appalled grey faces of old people peer through net curtains, afraid, because soon eggs will be thrown, and fireworks, and worse. The sirens have already started up down below. I walk back up towards the dark hump of

mountain and the little hunched house.

Mammy's watching the telly. She's drinking wine, all squashed up on the sofa wearing a frayed dressing gown and the bottom of her feet dirty. She likes those programmes where rich people buy a house in a hot country, and go round saying 'oh it's quite nice' and 'the kitchen's a bit small for entertaining' and 'oh look at the view.' Really boring. But tonight we're going to watch a film.

But just as Mammy starts to flick through to find the film, there's a noise in the hall. The letter-box is pushed open, a mouth breathing through. It's the brave boy, the chip shop boy. The fumble-fingered boy with sour vinegar breath and salty fingers. I shout at him through the closed door to go away and he shouts back that he just wants to tell me happy birthday. But then Mammy's behind me in the hall, pushing me aside, bending to spit at him through the letter-box.

'Get lost or I'll shove a sparkler up your arse.'

The letter-box slams shut. Mammy pulls at a reel of tape with her fingers, with her teeth, taping up the letterbox until it's criss-crossed like bandages on a cartoon wound. She doesn't know it's too late, that the chip shop boy already

planted a secret in my belly. She pours herself another glass of wine, sloshing it, and we sit with our chips and watch 'Mamma Mia' turned up really loud, both of us singing along. In the gaps between the songs we can hear the sound of scratching under the floor, quiet as rats. Mammy opens another bottle of wine because she knows you can keep chip shop boys out but there are some things you can't. Later, she cries at the happy ending and falls asleep with her mouth open in an anguished 'oh,' the glass toppled on her chest, the last drops of wine dribbling between her breasts.

I open my bedroom window and let the curtains blow just like on the night I was born, and listen to the lovely swoosh of the town, of shouting and sirens, radios and laughter, gulls and cars and something else too, deep down in the earth, a grinding, a pulse.

The scratching under the floor is louder now.

She's coming.

The night I was born I lay against Mammy's warm belly and watched as she and Daddy laughed together, bright like dream people. Mammy sipped tea, steam rising. She looked at me, her face very close, so beautiful she was, my Mammy. But then her smile changed to something else, her mouth opened wide. A mug smashed, hot brown liquid running, Mammy screaming.

'They've taken her! They've taken my baby!' She scrambled from the bed leaving trails of blood on the sheets behind her. Daddy darted to pull her back from the window, from the white curtains that framed the night. Mammy knew that They had come and she knew what They had done. But these things are not to be told, so Mammy was locked up until she stopped saying them, locked up with the silver-haired child who was not hers.

She's nearly here. She'll smell of the mountain. I'll take her out into the fogtime, and show her the lights and the smoke, the flashes of fireworks, the arch-backed cats, the teenagers hurling eggs. I'll show her the alleyway lovers with their wet kisses, the children with their chocolate-smeared faces, the shivering people outside pubs huddled in intimate clouds of smoke. I'll show her the city of fire with its flames reflected in the water and the dunes beyond it, and I'll show her the road where luminous cars streak past, the road that sounds like the sea. And then I'll show her the real sea, all silver in the mist and breathy.

And then I'll take her up the mountain, let her smell the gorse flowers, let her dig her fingers into soil, and we'll lie on the ground with our ears pressed into the earth and listen to the world below, the grind and toil of the world that was mine but is now hers. If she could stay with me I'd show her how clouds of starlings copy the shape of the dunes as they swoop along the shore at sunset. How, on a clear night, you can hear the song of the stars. How cats sleep on sunny days, stretched on warm walls. But as the grey light breaks she'll have to go, my dark-haired earth sister. She'll have to leave me and slip back underground.

And when she's gone I'll wait, for in time They'll come for my child too, and in its place They'll give me an infant, a fairy child. A changeling of my very own.

M.S. Corley

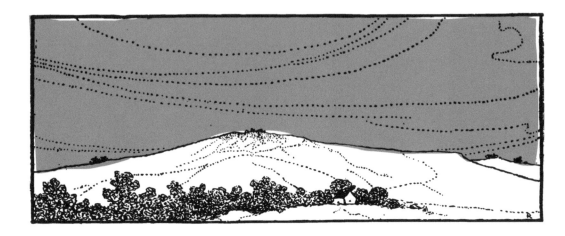

# THE HILL

## by Kristy Kerruish

"YOU ARE not seriously going through with it Trev?"

Jenny pulled up the car. It lurched over the soft puddles on the roadside and shuddered as she turned off the engine. The windscreen wipers slumped, the world beyond the windscreen turning to a smudge of greens and browns in seconds. There was nothing but the shallow pounding of the rain on the roof of the car.

Jenny prodded her phone into life and scrolled through her texts in irritation. "Seriously Trev? In this weather?"

"It's got to be tonight, it's Samhain."

"The daylight will be gone in half an hour."

"I have to know if there's any truth to Old Ben's story about what he saw that night. There's a piece in this."

Trevor meant that it was something he could write about: strange hauntings - thumps and bumps.

"You're wasting your time."

"I'll give it a minute to see if the rain goes off."

"You do know that it's all mumbo-jumbo, don't you? No self-respecting ghoul would be out in this weather."

Trevor peered through the window to the blurred green hill that rose up in front of them. "I'd better get on my way. The light is already fading." He showed her his map. "That's where we are and that hedge there, where the stile is, is an ancient boundary line."

Jenny gave him one of her exasperated looks.

"You're not coming then?" Trevor said with a smile, pulled on his rain jacket and stepped out, leaning in to take his camera bag up. He gave Jenny a wink and slammed the door shut. Jenny wiped the condensation from the window and looked at his diminishing figure as he stepped over the stile and trudged across the field.

Trevor had been gone for a while. The daylight had been gradually sucked away. Jenny tried to nudge her phone into life. It was dead. She found the charger and plugged it in. It remained blank and silent. Jenny frowned and clearing the condensation, peered at the dark mass of the hill ahead of her. The dusk was enveloping it, the hill had lost its colours as if they had run away in the rain.

Then a light pricked the darkness. A fire had been kindled on the hillside, a weak struggling flame fighting the rain. Over the next few minutes it grew with intensity and another appeared close by and then another. Gradually the hillside was lit with a constellation of lights; flickering fires.

Jenny stepped out of the car and, pulling her raincoat over her head, skirted gingerly around the puddles and raised herself up on the stile. She could see the fires more clearly now. The apparent flickering was caused by figures passing in front of them. Each fire had drawn a small crowd and now and then their shouts and laughter were driven on the wind towards her with the smell of woodsmoke. There were children nimbly running in and out of the dancing figures. She watched the silhouettes circling the fires for several minutes. There was a freedom and passion to

them, they danced around the flames with wild abandon, leaping and crying out. Some seemed to be wearing masks of gaping animal heads. She stepped over the stile and walked a little way through the wet grass, wondering if Trevor had found himself among the dancers. The only path up the hill would have taken him close to several of the bonfires. He might have stopped to warm himself and watch or scrounge a hamburger. The locals had a lot of spirit to come out on such a night but then, it was Halloween.

The pulse of the music was audible, drums and voices on the air, mesmerising; like a heartbeat. The dancers' bodies writhed with the rhythm, their voices throbbed with a repetitive phrase. Jenny took out her phone and tried to thumb it into life again. She raised it in the air but failed to find the elusive signal. Fortunately the torch still worked. The rain drops fell beaded in its weak light.

Suddenly there was a strange cry. It was as if some thing had screamed out in pain; a chill-ing, resonating sound like the scream of a fox in a snare. It seemed to hang in the air for several seconds before it faded into silence. Jenny froze when she heard it, pulled her hood back and faced into the rain, looking in the direction the sound came from in confusion. The figures had stopped their dancing and seemed to have turned – looking towards her. They must have seen the torch light. Gradually, like fireflies, smaller lights seemed to be swarming down the hillside. Sparks of light; flaming torches held and people running with them. Soon the torches reached the field and surged towards her. For a moment she saw nothing but streaks of colour, then the bushes heaved in front of her. Nothing was distinct, nothing had form.

Jenny turned and ran back to the car. In the darkness her feet found no purchase on the damp grass, they slid beneath her. She fell, scrambled to her feet, ran again without looking back, dancing over the puddles. The rain thickened, drumming on the foliage. She scrambled over the stile, 'a boundary line', she remembered Trevor's words. She was shaking so violently when she reached the car that for a moment she could hardly master her breathing and feel any sensation in her wet limbs. She clambered in and locked the doors and swore under her breath. The condensation masked the world outside. Fumbling to start the engine, she wiped the window but there was nothing on the hillside, the fires and dancers had gone.

A movement stirred in the twilight; Trevor's monochrome figure was coming towards the stile through the evening light. When he reached the car he knocked on the window, she opened the door and he pressed himself into the seat with a sigh.

Jenny sat in silence.

Trevor looked at her, her hair streaming and her trousers covered in wet mud. She was staring at the hill. It was in darkness. The night had swallowed everything.

"I don't know what I was hoping for really," Trevor sighed.

"What Trev? What exactly did Old Ben say?"

"That on this night, on Samhain, ghost fires burn on the hill. Ben saw people dancing, music and heard screams in the darkness. You were right Jen. It's all mumbo-jumbo," he smiled. "There's nothing up there."

Jenny said nothing. She started the engine with a shaking hand, looking up at the dark hill one last time through the beat of the wipers before turning onto the road.

# CONTRIBUTORS

**KRISTY KERRUISH** is originally from Edinburgh and currently lives in Europe. She writes fiction and poetry and has had work published online, in printed magazines and in books – including, among others, her short story 'Silence' in *Joe Stepped Off the Train and Other Stories*, edited by S. Kay in support of War Child.

**MARK SADLER** shares his home in Southend-on-Sea with a chameleon named Frederic. His writing has been performed by Liars' League in London and has appeared most recently on *The London Magazine* website and also on the Kaleidoscope Healthcare website as part of the *Writing the Future* summer reading anthology.

**DAMIEN B. RAPHAEL** began writing in 2010, having completed eight screenplays. I've also completed one novel and am taking a break on my second to try my hand at ghost stories, as I adore them.

**N.A. WILSON** has had two poems published by Forward Poetry: *Home of Aspirations* in The Great British Write Off, *Home is Where the Heart is anthology* (2014); *An Ode to the Spider and its Web in An Ode To anthology* (2014). A Flower in the Field of War was published as a flash fiction story in *Flash Fiction* (2015). This is his first foray into horror.

**CALLUM MCKELVIE** is a twenty-three year old lover of all things Gothic and grisly, doubtless due to his mother's influence, who delighted in telling him stories of Skeletons dancing in ruined graveyards whilst she played 'Danse Macabre'. He studied History at Aberystwyth University. He is currently unpublished, but writes reviews and articles for a number of genre fiction sites.

**FLORENCE VINCENT** is a writer based in Edinburgh, and a recent graduate of the University of Edinburgh's Creative Writing PhD. She writes stories straddling a variety of genres, but has a particular interest in the creepy, unsettling and downright bizarre. Her short fiction has been published in *Shoreline of Infinity* and *The Inkwell*.

**ALYS HOBBS** is a writer, illustrator and lover of all things ghostly and ghoulish. She lives in Derbyshire, where she works as a freelance Copywriter from her 200-year-old cottage. As well as holding a first-class degree in Creative Writing, she is also proud to have had several short stories published – most notably in *Popshot* magazine.

**CATRIN KEAN** is a Cardiff born writer who recently won a Bafta Cymru award for her short film 'Dad.' Her short stories have been published in *Riptide* and *Bridge House* anthologies as well as being shortlisted for the Fish prize. She is currently working on her first novel. She lives in Cardiff but can be more often found wandering the hills, forests and beaches of South Wales with her two ridgeback dogs.

**C. L. HANLON** was Louise Lloyd in a previous incarnation. Now living in Shrewsbury where she is studying an English degree. Her interests are books, writing and coffee, preferably all at the same time. She loves old graveyards, Victorian post-mortem photography, and the uncanny in everything.

**LEONA PRESTON** is an ardent Graphic Designer as well as a frenetic Illustrator! Occasionally she likes to write and specialises in character design.
*behance.net/leonapreston*

**M.S. CORLEY** is a freelance illustrator and graphic designer specializing in book covers and character design. His interests include Jesus, folklore, weird fiction, video games, monsters and the 19th Century. He's worked on everything from comic books to video game concept art, producing work for clients such as: Simon & Schuster, Thomas & Mercer, Crossing, Skyscape, 47North, Valancourt Books, Henry Holt Macmillan, Dark Horse Comics, Houghton Mifflin Harcourt, Microsoft and Penguin Random House. He lives with his wife, daughter, son and cat named Kanta in Central Oregon. Contact at: *corleyms@yahoo.com* Twitter: *@corleyms*

**REBECCA PARFITT** has worked in publishing for over a decade. Her debut poetry collection, *The Days After*, was published by Listen Softly London in 2017. She is a recipient of the Hay Festival Writers at Work residency and is currently working on a book of macabre short stories for which she won mentorship from Literature Wales. She lives in the Llynfi Valley, South Wales, with her partner and baby daughter.

**RHYS OWAIN WILLIAMS** is a writer and editor from Swansea, Wales. His first poetry collection, *That Lone Ship*, was published by Parthian in 2018. Rhys also runs *The Crunch* – a multimedia poetry magazine (*crunchpoetry.com*). In addition to all things ghastly, Rhys is interested by folklore, urban myth and psychogeography. He lives in a terraced house near the sea with his partner and a black cat named Poe.
*rhysowainwilliams.com*

**NATHANIEL WINTER-HEBERT** is the creative director at Winter-Hébert—a design studio tucked into the wilds of rural Québec, on the outskirts of Montreal. Nathaniel is inspired by modernist principles with an emphasis on typography, hierarchy, and concise, effective composition. In practice, he is fond of treading the magical middle zone between rationally driven design and the intuitive unknown.
*winterhebert.com*

Lightning Source UK Ltd.
Milton Keynes UK
UKHW051111180221
378942UK00003B/51

9 780993 499159